Enjoy!

love E

D0307137

(sorry about the colour pics!)

FRESH FROM THE SEA

FRESH FROM THE SEA

Fine Seafood Cooking

Michael Raffael

THE BODLEY HEAD
LONDON

Illustrations by Charles Shearer

A Jill Norman Book

A CIP catalogue record for this book
is available from the British Library

ISBN 0 370 31361 5
© Michael Raffael 1989
Illustrations © Charles Shearer

Photoset by Rowland Phototypesetting Limited,
Bury St Edmunds, Suffolk
Printed in Great Britain for
The Bodley Head Limited,
31 Bedford Square, London WC1B 3SG
by Butler and Tanner Limited, Frome and London

First published in 1989

Contents

Introduction

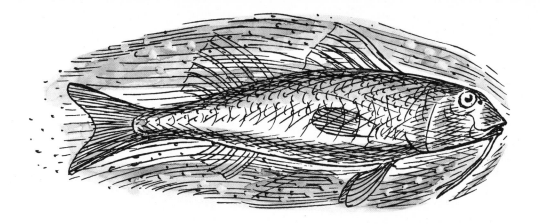

'A loaf of bread,' the Walrus said,
'Is what we chiefly need:
Pepper and vinegar besides
Are very good indeed –
Now, if you're ready, Oysters dear,
We can begin to feed.'

Through the Looking-glass by Lewis Carroll

Professional tasters have a specific vocabulary to describe the smell and taste of fish. At the top of their list they have terms such as 'strong seaweedy' and 'fresh and sweet'. Down at the bottom come 'faecal', 'ammonia' and 'putrid'. But it is the language describing mediocre quality which is more disturbing: 'boiled clothes', 'wood shavings', 'cotton wool'. Hardly less worrying is the seven to eight points meted out on a scale of ten to fish which is neutral, which has lost its characteristic taste, but not yet started to go off.

Very little of the fish sold over the counters of supermarkets or fishmongers would merit a top mark. Nor would much frozen fish. If the public wants to eat fish, it has to accept a compromise, it would seem.

Whereas meat, game and poultry all benefit from a shorter or longer delay between slaughter and eating, there has never been a demand for 'well-hung cod'.

Freshness is everything. Shellfish must be bought live if they are to be enjoyed to the full. Other fish have a longer or shorter life-in-death before they are fit only for the bin. Oily fish such as herring, sprat, whitebait and mackerel perish fastest. Sole or turbot may still be edible after a week depending on how they

I

have been handled. That is the crux of the matter. A Breton buying a lot of fish on the quayside will try to cheapen it by a sniffy criticism of *l'odeur de la cale*, the stench of the hold, implying that a writhing mass of mingled species has been left threshing and dying for the duration of the trawler's voyage at sea. It's the same smell which you find, though mitigated, outside even the most reputable fishmonger.

It's unfair to generalize and claim that a fish caught one day by an inshore fisherman is bound to be better than one that has lain on ice for a week, but it is more likely.

Take as an extreme case the angler who hires a boat for a day and goes out fishing for whiting. If the weather is cool and he catches nothing until an hour or so before he returns to shore, his catch will be pristine, better than anything that money can buy. Now assume that he goes out in a summer heatwave, catches a fish straightaway and leaves it lying ungutted on the deck for several hours. By the time that he pops his fillet into the pan for supper, it will hardly be better than the rockfish he could have bought from the local chippy.

It would be nice to say that the best way to buy fish is to find a sympathetic supplier and put yourself into his hands, but sooner or later you are going to be dissatisfied. The only way to purchase fish which is going to give you pleasure is to shop for it yourself and make your own decisions. The shops where you can buy fillets with confidence can be counted on the fingers of one hand. Wherever possible check the appearance of the whole fish before buying. The one infallible guide to freshness is a bright rounded eye. The converse is true too. Never buy a fish with sunken eyes. Prestige fishmongers boast a selection of exotic fish flown in from the Seychelles and so-called fresh red mullet. Look closely and you know that the limp, slimy specimens have lost their sweetness.

About ten years ago, I moved to the West Country and began buying a variety of fish from a family of inshore fishermen who had a couple of boats at Beer, on the south Devon coast. They would sell me monkfish and John Dory, minus their ugly, hefty heads for about 30p per pound. At the same time they were charging twice as much for plaice which they were forced to buy in from Brixham to meet the demand of their customers.

The sad thing was not that they were not reaping a fair reward for catching some of the most delicious fish in the sea, but that the customers wanted plaice and cod, whether it was fresh or a week old.

Things may be changing slowly. Restaurants snap up species such as John Dory, bass and monkfish and are prepared to pay a fair price for it, but they only sell a few portions a day to a small section of the public.

The Shellfish Association recently commissioned some market research into attitudes towards a variety of shellfish including scallops. Fewer than one in five of the population has ever eaten them and not many more would bother to try them, even given the opportunity. The researchers gave away samples and were disappointed that most of those who tried them could not understand what all the fuss was about. What the report failed to say was whether the scallops tried were fresh and how they had been prepared. If they were old or frozen after a prolonged polyphosphate bath, it is not surprising that few samplers were enthusiastic. Nobody is going to be converted to eating a new kind of fish overnight unless it is immediately recognized as being delicious. It is not the time to try and solve the vexed question as to what tastes good and what does not, but most of us have a deep-rooted atavistic love of seafood which has only been damaged by inferior quality and occasional outbreaks of food-poisoning, due for the most part to man-made pollution. Why else would millions of us go crazy over prawn cocktails made with insipid prawns and scampi which contain more rusk than fish?

When the Queen Mother was rushed to hospital with a salmon bone in her throat, the story made headline news. There is an irrational and mostly unwarranted fear of fish bones. There are species which are troublesome. Conger eel is an example. Its bones criss-cross the flesh in a sharp, hard-to-dislodge network. The tail end is particularly unpleasant. The best way of removing them is to cook the fish and pull out the bones with tweezers, but even this is not ideal. Other fish, like grey mullet, have sharp bones but they are easier to avoid. It is almost impossible to pursuade a generation of children brought up on fishfingers and baked beans to tackle a herring.

However, most fish, especially the flat fish, are not too hard to come to grips with. They do not require an advanced course in anatomy. Some seem to be better to eat if they are left intact. It would be hard to convince a scientist, but a sole appears to taste better on the bone. Perhaps it has something to do with the gelatinous film along the backbone. Sooner or later some 'enlightened' technologist is going to invent a way of extruding tapeworms of boneless, neutral fish with prawn flavour and revolutionize our eating habits. For the meanwhile, I prefer to be a heretic and enjoy my exercises in bone structure.

Many skilled chefs will tell you that they prefer cooking fish to meat because it allows more scope for their creative instincts. That may be so; nouvelle cuisine has come up with some delicious and frivolous creations over the last decade. In the name of exalted simplicity and respect for the produce, it has also had its share of unhappy marriages. The two French journalists who coined the 'nouvelle cuisine' tag wrote in their joint autobiography how they dined in the evening at the restaurant of Paul Bocuse and were served a red mullet and a few green beans. Like the fashion designer who dictates the season's hemlines, they launched the style on the strength of the experience. The ploy was astute because it had an element of truth underlying it, namely, that nothing beats fresh food simply prepared; boiled lobster outclasses *homard thermidor* any day. But there is plenty of scope left to the cook without the need to be arch, or over-elaborate or selfconsciously simple.

There are only two kinds of cooking: good and bad. Cooking a turbot or a mackerel requires little more skill, perhaps less, than boiling an egg. The latter requires you to cook the white so that it is set and to leave the yolk runny. With a fish you only have to worry about the flesh.

So what constitutes well cooked? The Japanese eat raw fish because they are confident about its freshness and flavour. Europeans are less confident about raw fish, though the Dutch and Scandinavians eat herrings this way and in a variety of guises. Smoked salmon is actually raw, flavoured rather than cooked by the smoke. There has been a trend towards cooking fish as though it were a medium-done steak, i.e. set on the surface and raw in the centre. That trick doesn't often work, not to my taste anyway. It's not much fun scraping at raw flesh tangled around the backbone. At the other extreme, a dry overcooked fish has the texture of cotton wool or cardboard depending on the species. The critical area between cooked, overcooked and undercooked is narrow. Take monkfish as an example. Dry, it is unattractive, a boring fish. Cooked, it is firm, sweet and delicious. Rare, it is slimy and very much an acquired taste.

Whether you use oil, water, steam or an oven to reach the right degree of cooking is immaterial. It is the ability to recognize that point and achieve it that counts. Although it is not often expressed, there is a good deal of scorn felt by professional cooks for 'amateurs'. It is based on a feeling that the pro has an armoury of techniques which are inaccessible to the uninitiated.

Unlike cooking a large joint of meat, preparing a fish involves short times. For this reason, be suspicious of any recipe which states categorically 'Seal for 4½ minutes'. Your pan, your fat, your heat, may all be different from that of the person who supplied the recipe you are following. It is far better to trust your nose, eyes, ears and intelligence.

The recipes in this book were prepared over a number of years, when I was tired or happy or 'inspired' or bored or cooking a routine meal for the family. Some are part of a repertoire that is re-used from time to time. Others are not, merely the froth of an hour or so spent dabbling in the kitchen. On the whole they are pretty honest. Some, in my opinion, would be worth a detour for the most critical foodie gourmet.

**All the recipes are for 4
unless otherwise stated**

4

Fresh off the Beach

sea beet · samphire · sea kale

Then there are the wild originals whose flavour has unfamiliar intensity and still bears the character of the original habitat — sea beet and rock samphire, for example.

'Wild Things' by Tom Jaine in *Petits Propos Culinaires* 15 (1983)

Beneath the rampart of crumbling chalk which hides the Undercliffe, that secret garden of nature stretching from Lyme to Axmouth, is an untidy shorescape of shattered rockpools, shingle and weed-strewn ledges.

Hidden among its crannies live colonies of mussels, outnumbered by the massive winkle population. There is not too much a cook can do to a winkle; drop it in boiling water and pick it with a bent safety pin, or make a soup or preserve it in vinegar. But the mussels, that's a different matter altogether. They are not large; few measure more than my little finger, but they are unpolluted, free of barnacles for the most part and none too gritty. Despite their diminutive size, they are plump, juicy and sweet.

Nobody has ever bettered the classic mussel recipe, Moules marinière. Diced onions and shallots soften in a shivering haze of butter. Into the pan go a few parsley stalks and a glass of boiling *gros plant* or other inexpensive white wine. Then it's the turn of the mussels. In a couple of shakes they start to gape and are ready for eating. The trick is not to overfill the pan; you must coax them to open in unison. Afterwards sprinkle them with roughly chopped parsley, but not the powdery green dust beloved of some chefs. At best it's tasteless, at worst bitter.

A rarer treat, but worth trying as a star turn at a beach picnic, is the Charentes Maritime speciality, *éclade*. Arrange mussels tightly packed on a trencher or plank. Pile dried pine needles over the top and set them alight. The flash-fire is enough to cook the molluscs. Avoid doing this on pebble stones and you will please the conservationists. Fire will shatter flintstones.

Seaweed eating may appear to all Europeans bar the Welsh as a Japanese aberration. *Wakame, nori* and *kombu* don't slip off the tongue with familiarity for most of us, but the stampede to find new recipes has driven cooks to experiment with algae. Shellfish soup with sea lettuce (*ulva lactuca*), mussel, almond and seaweed soup, oysters poached with sea lettuce, seaweed-wrapped bass, seaweed and artichoke salad and a jellied fish and seaweed stew are just a few dishes which have found their way on to menus and into print.

Jacques Le Divellec, who earned his reputation in La Rochelle before moving to Paris to cash in on it, bottles a seaweed vinegar. It has a subtle iodine flavour which makes it ideal for seafood salads. A homemade version is easy to prepare and just as good (see page 8). It also seems a good idea to use seaweed when barbecuing fish. Dry the weeds and toss them on to the coals just before adding the bass, mackerel or mullet. Popweed is especially effective, as is the frilly sweet oar weed. The crackle does more for the imagination than the taste. Sea beet grows at the rim of the shoreline just beyond the reach of the high tide. Unlike many wild vegetables it has a taste akin to its domestic cousin, spinach. Comparing the two is like measuring wild sorrel against its kitchen garden counterpart. The leaves are tougher; they do not break down when boiled and the taste is both cleaner and sharper.

Rock samphire and marsh samphire can grow within feet of each other. At the mouth of the river Axe they do. Yet the plants belong to separate families.

Marsh samphire is a member of the *salicorniae*. Its spongy spikes grow in clumps on tidal mud flats and in salt marshes. The stalks binding the fronds together like a fine thread tend to give them a stringy feel in the mouth, but when steamed or poached, marsh samphire has a unique texture and taste. It is supposed to be picked after the longest day of the year, but I like to gather it very young early in summer, when the tips first emerge from the ground and the threads which hold the structure together have not had a chance to develop.

Rock samphire (the name is an anglicized form of *herbe de St Pierre*) grows on rocks, cliffs and in the cracks of old sea walls, or even in estuaries. As distinct from marsh samphire it has less spongy, succulent leaves; they're rather like well-fleshed dill. To taste, it is more perfumed than marsh samphire, but it does not have the stringy links – it's a bit like eating chrysanthemums. Their tangy scent makes them off-putting in large quantities even if you like the taste. I first picked it on Jersey, took it back to the hotel where I was staying and cooked it, with the manager's permission, at midnight after eating a very good dinner. In the 18th century both rock and marsh samphire were pickled. Where it seems wholly appropriate that St Peter's herb should be plunged into an acid bath, it seems rather a shame to overpower marsh samphire with the same treatment.

Mussels in Cider

30 g / 1 oz butter
115 g / 4 oz finely diced shallots
a few parsley stalks
2 tablespoons chopped parsley
200 ml / 7 fl oz medium dry
farmhouse cider
2 tablespoons chicken stock
1.25 litres / 1 quart mussels

Literally a stone's throw from the entrance to Axmouth harbour, there are a couple of small mussel colonies; small in both senses. Many of them are not much bigger than a lady's fingernail. They are, however, delectably sweet and tender, and relatively free from grit and sand because they grow among the boulders below the cliff.

The trick with mussels is to cook only as many at one time as the pan can comfortably hold. That way they are all cooked at the same time.

Melt the butter in a large *rondeau* (a kind of sawn-off saucepan with straight sides about 3 inches deep). Add the shallots and parsley stalks. Stew over a low heat until the shallots become transparent. Stir in the chopped parsley, cider and chicken stock. Bring to the boil. Add the mussels to the pan. Cover. Turn up the heat. After 1 minute, remove the lid and continue cooking until all the mussels have opened. This may take another couple of minutes.

NOTE: there are still dozens of farmhouses in the West Country producing cider. Julian Temperley of Burrow Hill near Langport is among the best. The Fruit and Cider Institute at Long Ashton outside Bristol makes artificially carbonated cider which nonetheless has a strong apple aroma.

Fried Mussels

1 egg, separated
1 tablespoon sunflower or
groundnut oil
1 tablespoon lager
50 ml / 2 fl oz water
80 g / 3 oz flour
250 g / 9 oz shelled cooked
mussels
salt
oil for frying

The following recipe is for a batter made with lager. Beat an egg yolk with the oil. Add the lager, the water, the flour and a pinch of salt. Whip the egg white until it is frothy and risen but not too firm. Fold it into the batter. Heat the frying oil. Dip the mussels in the batter one at a time and drop them into the hot oil. They should be fried in about 3 minutes if the oil is hot enough. Drain on absorbent paper and sprinkle with salt.

NOTE: mussels cooked as for Moules marinière are best for this recipe.

Sea Kale—the Lost Vegetable

'On many parts of the sea coast,' wrote the naturalist William Curtis, 'especially of Devon, Dorset and Sussex, the inhabitants from time immemorial have been in the practice of procuring it [sea kale] for their tables preferring it to all other greens.'

Curtis's tract on *crambe maritima* appeared in 1799. At that time, he pointed out, every gentleman in Devon had a sea kale plantation in the garden. He was probably right. Early seed catalogues list it among the cultivated edible plants.

Sea kale is similar to Belgian chicory and the French Argenteuil asparagus in that it must be kept out of the daylight to give of its best.

It grows naturally in deep shingle. In the early spring little tufts appear among the pebbles. They have to be excavated to a depth of a few inches so as to reveal the white stalks of the sea kale. This is the edible part. The leaves are bitter. Curtis suggested that it should be served on toast with 'melted butter', which at that date could either be simply that, or hollandaise sauce.

'Twenty minutes boiling,' advised Curtis, 'is sufficient to make it tender, but it is done in less.' Nowadays we cook our vegetables for less time than we did and half that time, depending on the thickness of the stalks, should be plenty.

He also says a final and conclusive word in sea kale's favour: 'It does not impart to the urine that unpleasant smell which [asparagus] is well known to do.'

Seaweed Vinegar

80 g / 3 oz assorted seaweeds
900 ml / 1 ½ pints white wine or spirit vinegar

Rinse the seaweed (mixed edible weeds such as kelp, bladderwrack, dulse, sea lettuce, oar weed). Pour boiling water over them, leave to stand 1 minute and drain. Put them in a jar. Cover with boiling vinegar. Leave to stand a few days before using. Properly sealed, this will keep for over a year and the flavour seems to improve with age.

Rock Samphire Salad

50 g / 2 oz pine kernels
115 g / 4 oz rock samphire
1 cabbage lettuce
4 tablespoons olive oil
fresh lime juice
salt

Toast the pine kernels in a non-stick pan over a low heat until they are well coloured.

Blanch the samphire for 2 minutes in boiling salted water and drain.

Pick and wash the yellow leaves in the heart of the lettuce. Mix the olive oil, lime juice and salt. Combine with the other salad ingredients and toss them *'comme un fou'*.

NOTE: if you go on a samphire picking expedition, select only the tender young tips.

Baby Skate with Rock Samphire

150 g / 5 oz rock samphire
1 tablespoon tarragon mustard
2 tablespoons wine vinegar
6 tablespoons groundnut or
    sunflower oil
2 tablespoons diced shallots
salt
4 × 175 g / 6 oz skate wings,
    skinned
50 g / 2 oz clarified butter
pepper

Choose the more tender tops of rock samphire. Drop them in boiling unsalted water and simmer for 3–4 minutes. Drain and rinse under the cold tap. Make a dressing with mustard, vinegar, oil, shallots and salt. Drop the samphire in the vinaigrette and leave to stand for 2 hours.

Trim the skate wings (they should be skinned both sides). Heat the butter in a large pan. Stew the skate in butter, turning the wings after 3–4 minutes. Turn up the heat so they brown a little on one side.

Arrange on four plates. Discard the butter in the pan. Add the vinaigrette and samphire. Grind lots of pepper over it. Swirl the vinaigrette around in the hot pan and pour over the skate wings.

Fillets of Whiting with Marsh Samphire

4 × 175 g / 6 oz whiting fillets
salt, pepper
175 g / 6 oz marsh samphire
50 g / 2 oz clarified butter
150 ml / ¼ pint double cream
1 tablespoon chopped parsley
2 teaspoons malt whisky

The most tender marsh samphire is the first of the year which starts to come up at the end of May.

Skin the whiting. Sprinkle the fillets with salt, leave them for an hour then pat dry.

If the samphire is mature separate the succulent tips from the fibrous network holding them together. Wash, and remove traces of weed. Drop into unsalted boiling water. Simmer 2–3 minutes, drain and reserve.

Heat the butter in a pan. Sauté the fillets 1 minute either side over a high flame. Drain most of the fat from the pan, deglaze it with cream. Stir in the samphire, reduce the sauce to a light coating consistency and season. Stir in the parsley and whisky.

Whiting Fillets with Sea Beet

4 × 175 g / 6 oz whiting fillets
sea salt
175 g / 6 oz sea beet
4 eggs
1 teaspoon vinegar
50 g / 2 oz butter
150 ml / ¼ pint double cream
nutmeg
chopped parsley

Sprinkle sea salt over the whiting and leave them for an hour. Pat dry. Pull out any tough stalks from the sea beet. Cook the leaves 5 minutes in boiling salted water. Drain and press out excess water.

Poach the eggs in boiling water to which you have added the vinegar. Drain and trim the eggs. Melt the butter in a pan. Sauté the whiting fillets 1 minute either side. Remove and keep hot. Discard most of the fat in the pan. Add the sea beet and cream to the pan. Season with a pinch of salt and nutmeg. Boil for 1 minute.

Arrange the sea beet on four plates, with the eggs on top. Lay the whiting fillets alongside and sprinkle with chopped parsley.

NOTE: a good trick for making the white adhere to the yolk when poaching eggs is to turn the boiling water into a whirlpool by stirring vigorously. Then drop in the egg and the white sets round the yolk.

Sea Purslane Salad

115 g / 4 oz sea purslane
50 g / 2 oz marsh samphire
sea salt
50 g / 2 oz seeded and diced
    cucumber
2 slices wholemeal bread
50 ml / 2 fl oz olive oil
1 clove garlic, cut in two
½ teaspoon Dijon mustard
1 tablespoon seaweed vinegar
1 teaspoon diced shallots
1 tablespoon walnut oil
50 g / 2 oz carrots, grated

Blanch the sea purslane 1 minute in boiling water. Drain and dry. Blanch the samphire in the same way for 2 minutes. Salt the cucumber, leave for 30 minutes. Rinse and pat dry. Remove the crusts and cube the slices of bread; fry in the oil, reserving 2 tablespoons of it. Rub the golden croûtons with garlic and grind sea salt over them.

Make a dressing with the remaining oil, mustard, seaweed vinegar, shallots, walnut oil and some salt.

Toss the vegetables, including the carrot, in the dressing. Sprinkle the croûtons over them and serve.

Grey Mullet Baked with Wild Fennel

1 × 1.35 kg / 3 lb grey mullet
50 g / 2 oz melted butter
2 stalks wild fennel
2 tablespoons chopped wild
    fennel leaves
1 tablespoon chopped parsley
½ lemon
salt, pepper

Grey mullet does not receive the respect it deserves, partly because it is compared unfavourably with red mullet to which it is not related, partly because fish caught in river estuaries can taste muddy and partly because its bones, though not hard to locate, are sharp and daunting. It is advisable to scrape away the tough scales of mullet before baking it, though not essential, because the skin is too tough to eat with much enthusiasm.

Clean and season the mullet inside and out. Brush a sheet of foil with the butter. Put the fennel stalks inside the fish. Sprinkle the fennel leaves and parsley over it. Squeeze the lemon over it and add the remaining butter, salt and plenty of freshly ground black pepper. Wrap up the foil parcel and bake the mullet for 45 minutes at 190°C, 375°F, gas mark 5. You can serve the mullet at once or let it cool and serve with a classic mayonnaise made with egg yolk and olive oil.

Stuffed Sprats

450 g / 1 lb sprats
2 tablespoons chopped fennel
    leaves
1 clove garlic, crushed
1 shallot, diced
½ lemon
50 g / 2 oz breadcrumbs
salt
50 ml / 2 fl oz groundnut or
    sunflower oil

Is it really worth the trouble of filleting 30 or 40 sprats so that you can stuff them with flavoured breadcrumbs? If you are handy with a knife and have a spare half hour, then perhaps.

Split the sprats head to tail and cut off their heads. Throw away the guts. Rinse the fish. Flatten one by one to loosen the backbones. Pull them out leaving the fish otherwise intact.

Combine the fennel, garlic, shallot and grated lemon zest. Stir in the juice of the lemon with the crumbs, a little salt and the oil.

Sprinkle about a teaspoon of the mixture over each opened fillet. Roll them up. Arrange them fairly closely packed on a greased baking tray. Brush with oil and bake 10 minutes in a hot oven, 220°C, 425°F, gas mark 7.

Braised School Bass

4 × 450 g / 1 lb bass
50 g / 2 oz unsalted butter
salt, pepper
80 g / 3 oz sliced baby carrots
80 g / 3 oz sliced leeks
80 g / 3 oz finely sliced onion
½ teaspoon lemon thyme
115 ml / 4 fl oz fish consommé
  (page 80)

Bass more than salmon or seatrout are a long time in the growing. A 10 pound fish may be 8 or 9 years old. The young fish are known as school, or sometimes club bass. They are a fisherman's fish, and few find their way to market. Along the Devon coast are some favourite spots of bass anglers. One is Seatown, near Bridport, where an outcrop of flat rock forms a small lagoon close inshore. Anglers fish with fly rods and spinners and haul their catch over the rocks into calm water before landing them.

Brush the bass with butter and season them. Melt the rest of the butter in a pan and stew the carrot, leek and onion. When they start to soften, transfer them to an ovenproof dish. Rub the fish with the lemon thyme, then put them on top. Pour over the consommé. Cover the fish and bake 15 minutes in a hot oven, 200°C, 400°F, gas mark 6. Turn the fish and braise for 5 more minutes. (If the consommé was cool to start with, cooking may take longer.)

Bass, Weeds and Winkles

1 kg / 2¼ lb approx. seaweed
600 ml / 1 pint approx. winkles
1 kg / 2¼ lb bass
1 shallot, diced
2 tablespoons dry white wine
300 ml / ½ pint double cream

On a trip to the seaside collect some edible seaweed—kelp, dulse, bladderwrack etc. Also collect a small bucket of winkles and rinse them in seawater.

Put a layer of weed in the bottom of a large cocotte or oven dish and strew with half the winkles. Lay the cut of bass taken from the middle of a large fish on top. Cover with any weeds you may have left. Pour over 300 ml / ½ pint of boiling water, cover the pan and bake the fish 20 minutes in a hot oven, 220°C, 425°F, gas mark 7. It may take a few minutes longer, so check and return to the oven if necessary.

While the fish is cooking drop the remaining winkles into a pan of boiling salted water. Return to the boil, skim the surface and take the pan off the heat. Pick as many of the winkles as your patience allows. Keep 150 ml / ¼ pint of their cooking liquor.

Reduce this liquor with the shallot and wine. Add the cream and boil to a light coating consistency. Pull off the black intestines at the end of the winkles and add the edible parts to the sauce.

Take the bass from the oven. Lay it on a heated serving dish with some of the weed for decoration only and serve the sauce separately.

Roast Bass with Flageolets

1 × 1.6 kg / 3½ lb bass
1 tablespoon groundnut oil
50 g / 2 oz butter
1 sprig + 1 tablespoon chopped savory
salt, pepper
220 g / 8 oz flageolets
30 g / 1 oz diced green streaky bacon, rind removed
1 dried chilli, diced
1 teaspoon chopped sage
30 g / 1 oz grated Cheddar

Scale and clean the bass. Brush the outside with oil. Put a little of the butter inside together with a sprig of savory, salt and pepper. Boil the flageolets in salted water for upwards of an hour, until tender. Drain.

Bake the bass 25 minutes in a hot oven, 220°C, 425°F, gas mark 7.

Melt the remaining butter in a pan, add the bacon and stew for a couple of minutes over a low heat. Stir in the chilli, savory and sage. Cook for 2 minutes more. Sauté the beans in the herbs and butter and mix in the Cheddar.

Serve the bass whole on a bed of flageolets.

NOTE: if you find this dish on the dry side, you can serve it with cream flavoured with lemon juice, salt and pepper; yoghurt flavoured with herbs or a 60–40 blend of mayonnaise and yoghurt flavoured with herbs.

Scallops

scallop

But now fresh scallops are sold without their shells. This is because scallops are sold by weight and the weight of the shell is as much or more than its contents.

Colin Spencer's *Fish Cookbook*

Tucked safe inside its clamped shell, the scallop abides in peace and good health. Scrape it off the seabed, leave it lying in a shop window for a few hours and it will start to yawn with discomfort. Eventually it will die. Thereafter, it decays rapidly. A fishmonger who obliges his customers by cutting the mollusc from its elegant striate mansion performs an even greater disservice. By killing it at once, he virtually guarantees that it will have lost its sweetness before it reaches the rich man's table (you need to be rich to afford scallops).

And what of frozen scallops, swollen in their plastic packages which sweat and leach out their added water as they defrost? Commercially transformed into sponges with the help of polyphosphates, they have long lost the original succulence which makes them such a delicacy.

It's hard to grasp why a nation which used to swallow tens of millions of live oysters every year should treat scallops with such ignorance and lack of culinary sympathy. 'Cook [scallops] in a very moderate oven,' wrote Dorothy Hartley in her classic *Food in England*. 'They will take about forty minutes, perhaps longer if large.' In that length of time the tender meat will have dried and hardened to a white rubber bullet before the connective tissues start to break down.

Scallops, depending on their size, cook in a couple of minutes. They can even be eaten raw. Eventhia Senderens, wife of Alain, one of the *vedettes* of modern French cuisine, has a scallop recipe for six-month-old babies: 'Halve a large scallop, poach it one minute either side in 5 cl of water. Drain the pieces and reduce the liquid by half. Off the heat, beat a knob of butter the size of a hazelnut into the juices. Liquidize the scallop and its sauce and serve with a carrot purée.'

Perhaps the reason why the British have not taken to scallops when they are willing to swallow vinegary cockles and winkles lies with the fishermen. Dredging the rocky sea-floor is one of the dirtiest and most tiring jobs. In Lyme Bay they go out scalloping when they need the money, usually in November, when the weather is clement.

The location of well-stocked beds has to be a jealously guarded secret. A few years ago, some of the large Brixham boats got wind of the fact that Beer fishermen had been bringing in large quantities of scallops. They spied on their smaller rivals, discovered where the bed was and scraped it clean within a week.

Smaller Queen scallops, which have two concave shells rather than one flat and one rounded, are still quite abundant. The fishermen bring them up in the trawl, but they toss them back into the sea which is a shame, because they are also good to eat.

In cool weather, a scallop will live for several days out of the water if covered with damp sacking. If you are not going to trust the fishmonger to open your scallops, you must learn how to do it yourself. Live, they are very sensitive. Put a knife between the shells without due care and you may find it caught tight. Choose a very thin bladed fish-filleting knife. Introduce the point through the chink where the narrow rectangular end meets the curved part of the shell. Keeping the knife pressed flush against the flat shell, detach the scallop from it. Pull away the bottom shell and remove the scallop from the rounded shell either with a spoon or with your knife.

The diaphanous beard around the scallop is edible, but most cooks throw it away. If you are frugal keep it for fish stock. Remove the black intestine running round the scallop's girth and the black sac, but keep the coral.

You may have to rinse away grit and sand, but never leave scallops to soak since they lose their flavour.

For many years the only scallop recipe which had any credence with professional chefs was Coquilles Saint-Jacques. Scallops were cooked, popped into the round shell, covered in white béchamel sauce and cooked au gratin. The apostles of nouvelle cuisine, whatever their faults, realized that this method masked the flavour. Ever since, recipes ranging from imaginative or bizarre to inspired have evolved for this juicy morsel. The simplest way is still the best. Put your scallops in a small pan and cover them with seawater. (You are allowed to do this in England; in France seawater used to belong to the Crown and, probably, belongs to the Republic these days.) Heat the water to simmering point. Leave the scallops for a couple of minutes, drain them and brush them with a little butter.

A word of warning about the shells. They are porous. It is quite safe to use them to present the scallops once. If you intend to keep and recycle them for presenting other dishes, they need to be washed *and* sterilized or they could cause a nasty dose of poisoning.

Roast Scallops in their Shells

8 scallops
220 g / 8 oz flour
115 g / 4 oz slightly salted
  butter
salt, pepper
4 mint leaves
½ lemon, finely sliced

Open and clean scallops. Discard the flat shells. Mix a little water with the flour to make a stiffish paste.

Pour the melted butter into 4 concave scallop shells. Lay 2 scallops in each one. Season with salt and pepper. Finely chop the mint and sprinkle over the scallops. Lay a very thin slice of lemon on each pair of scallops. Divide the dough into four and roll each bit into a long, thin band. Lay the bands around the circumference of the scallop shells. Plant a second concave shell on the one containing the scallops. Press down so that the dough seals the shells together.

Bake 10 minutes in a very hot oven, 220°C, 425°F, gas mark 7. Serve the shells as they are; they can easily be prised apart with a knife. If you are worried about them wobbling about on the dinner plates, balance them on a small mound of rice or mashed potato.

Scallops with Celeriac Soubise and Toasted Almonds

350 g / 12 oz peeled and
  chopped celeriac
115 g / 4 oz sliced onion
30 g / 1 oz butter
300 ml / ½ pint milk
salt
50 g / 2 oz skinned almonds
12 scallops
2 tablespoons almond oil
pepper

Put the celeriac, onion, butter, milk and a little salt in a pan. Simmer gently until the celeriac and onion are soft and tender. Liquidize the vegetables with their cooking liquor to obtain a thickish sauce.

Toast the almonds in a hot oven until they brown, and sprinkle with salt.

Shell, clean and halve the scallops. Heat the almond oil in a large pan. Quickly fry the scallops. Season. Arrange the scallops on a bed of soubise and garnish with the toasted almonds.

16

Steamed Scallops with Saffron-flavoured Peppers

115 g / 4 oz finely diced onion
15 g / ½ oz butter
1 tablespoon olive oil
¼–½ teaspoon chilli powder
2 teaspoons lemon juice
2 teaspoons tomato purée
350 g / 12 oz red capsicums
1 tablespoon dry white vermouth
2 sachets saffron
salt, pepper
12 scallops

Sweat the onion in butter and olive oil. When it becomes transparent add the chilli powder, lemon juice and tomato purée. Add the capsicums cut in strips, white vermouth and saffron dissolved in a little hot water. Season, cover the pan and simmer 15 minutes. Remove the lid and continue to stew until most of the liquid has evaporated.

Shell, clean and halve the scallops. Lay them on top of the piping hot pepper bed. Cover and steam 3 minutes. Turn and steam 1 more minute.

NOTE: chilli powder can vary considerably in strength. Use enough to give a sharp note to the dish, but not a fiery taste. According to one account 85% of all saffron is adulterated, so that it is difficult to give exact proportions. Two 1-gram sachets of genuine Spanish saffron will give a distinctive aroma to the peppers.

Poached Scallops with Jersey Royal New Potatoes

12 scallops
700 g / 1½ lb Jersey Royals
300 ml / ½ pint fish stock
2 tablespoons seaweed vinegar (page 8)
6 tablespoons groundnut oil
2 teaspoons chopped chervil
salt, pepper
40 g / 1½ oz diced shallots

Shell, clean and slice the scallops into three. Wash and scrub the Jersey Royals. Boil them in salted water until tender. The time will depend on their size and freshness.

Put the scallops in the cold, light fish stock. Bring to the boil over moderate heat and drain them at once.

Make a dressing with the vinegar, oil, chervil and seasoning.

Slice the potatoes thickly and toss them with the shallots in three-quarters of the dressing. Spoon them on to four plates or into four bowls. Put the scallops on top and coat with the remaining dressing. Grind some extra black pepper over them. Serve warm.

Poached Scallops with Sour Cream and Chive Sauce

Clean a dozen scallops and put them in a small pan with 300 ml / ½ pint of cold fish stock. Bring slowly to the boil, then take out the scallops. Pour half of the stock into a clean pan and reduce it rapidly to about 3 tablespoons. Add a teaspoon of armagnac and a hint of cayenne pepper. Whisk in 150 ml / ¼ pint of thick sour cream. Stir in 2 tablespoons of chopped chives. Check the seasoning. Heat thoroughly but do not boil. Spoon over the scallops.

Minted Scallops

Serves 2
1 large ridge cucumber
salt
1 tablespoon white wine vinegar
2 teaspoons chopped mint
1 pinch icing sugar
6 scallops
50 g / 2 oz butter
4 shallots, diced
1 tablespoon chopped parsley
corn salad to garnish

Peel and seed the cucumber; cube and salt it. Leave it to drain 1 hour, then rinse. Poach 4 minutes and refresh under cold water. Drain well.

Combine vinegar, mint and icing sugar. Shell, clean and halve the scallops. Melt half the butter in a pan. Fry the scallops in the butter. Lay them in circles on two plates. Keep hot.

Put the shallots in the pan in which the scallops were cooked. Fry 1 minute then add the minted vinegar and the cucumber and shake until the cucumber is well-coated. Put the remaining butter in the pan and shake well so that it forms a light emulsion. Pour the sauce over the scallops and sprinkle with chopped parsley.

You can decorate the outside of the plate with corn salad. Fancy greengrocers charge an arm and a leg for it, but you may well find it growing wild in your garden. It has the advantage of flourishing in early winter when the range of salads greens can be boring.

Scallops with Sautéed Jerusalem Artichokes

1 tablespoon flour
salt, pepper
450 g / 1 lb Jerusalem artichokes
   (peeled weight)
30 g / 1 oz butter
1 tablespoon olive oil
12 scallops
1 tablespoon chopped parsley

For the sauce:
1 egg yolk
1 teaspoon Dijon mustard
1 dessertspoon wine vinegar
150 ml / ¼ pint olive oil
2 teaspoons chopped capers
1 teaspoon each of chopped
   parsley, tarragon and chives
1 dill cucumber, chopped

Whisk the flour into a pan of boiling salted water. Add the artichokes, simmer 10 minutes and drain them.

Heat the butter and olive oil in a frying pan and sauté the artichokes until they start to colour.

Shell, clean and halve the scallops. Add them to the pan and sauté 2 minutes more. Season and sprinkle with chopped parsley.

Serve with a classic rémoulade sauce: prepare a mayonnaise with egg yolk, mustard, vinegar and oil. Season and stir in capers, herbs and the dill cucumber.

Steamed Scallops and Warm Cabbage Vinaigrette

8 scallops
salt
½ Savoy cabbage, finely chopped
¼ lemon
4 small carrots, grated
2 shallots, diced
2 tablespoons *vieux vinaigre de vin*
7 tablespoons groundnut oil

Should it be *vieux vinaigre de vin* or rather *vinaigre de vin vieux?* You can see both forms on labels of old wine vinegar. But not all old wine vinegar is of the same quality and it's really a case of the more it costs the better it is likely to be.

Shell, clean and halve the scallops. Steam them 4 minutes and season lightly. Cook the cabbage in boiling salted water for a few minutes until tender. Drain and express as much of the water as you can. Squeeze the lemon juice over the carrots.

Beat the shallots with the vinegar, oil and salt. Spoon some of this vinaigrette over the scallops and the rest over the cabbage.

Arrange the cabbage on four plates and decorate with scallops. Sprinkle carrot over the top. Serve while still tepid if possible.

19

Sautéed Scallops with Malt Whisky and a Julienne of Vegetables

12 scallops
50 g / 2 oz each of carrot, swede, parsnip, young turnip, celeriac and sweet potato
salt, pepper
30 g / 1 oz butter
1 teaspoon fresh thyme leaves
2 tablespoons malt whisky

Shell, clean and halve the scallops. Cut the carrot, swede, parsnip, young turnip, celeriac and sweet potato into matchstick-sized strips. Boil 3 minutes in salted water and drain. (If you are a perfectionist you should cook these vegetables in separate pans.)

Heat the butter in a pan with the thyme leaves. Add the scallops and sauté 2 minutes. Pour in the malt whisky (something smooth rather than an Islay type of malt, e.g. Glenlivet, Glenmorangie or Macallan). Stir the scallops until they are impregnated with the whisky. Stir in the vegetables and season.

NOTE: not having all the different vegetables to hand is no reason for not trying this recipe. The important ones are the carrot, celeriac, swede and parsnip.

Spinach and Scallop Bonne Bouche

450 g / 1 lb leaf spinach
salt
1 shallot, finely diced
50 g / 2 oz butter
1 tablespoon double cream
about 175 g / 6 oz smoked haddock fillet
4 scallops

Wash the spinach thoroughly and remove any tough stalks. Sprinkle with salt and put in a pan over a moderate heat. Cook for a few minutes in the water clinging to the leaves until tender, turning it once or twice to cook evenly. Drain, and press out all excess moisture.

Stew the shallot in some of the butter until transparent. Add the cream. Combine with the spinach. Keep hot in a shallow pan.

Carve 4 slices from the haddock. (Make sure it has not been dyed with tartrazine. Tartrazine is often a garish yellow paint on the haddock's surface, but it can also be no more than a dirty stain. Good Finnan haddock is hardly coloured at all by the smoking; it has an off-white tinge.) Lay the slices on the spinach and cover the pan. Cook over a gentle heat just long enough for the haddock to steam. Meanwhile, shell and clean the scallops. Sauté them over a high heat in the remaining butter until they are slightly coloured.

To serve, arrange a neat pile of spinach in the centre of a warmed medium-sized plate with a slice of haddock on it. Put a scallop on top.

Scallops and Toasted Cheese

12 scallops
2 tablespoons groundnut oil
175 g / 6 oz grated unpasteurized
 Cheddar
cayenne pepper

This is much too rich to serve as part of a dinner running to several courses, but as a snack it is very good.

Shell and clean the scallops and sauté over a high heat in the oil.

Preheat the grill. Put the scallops on small plates. Sprinkle the Cheddar over the scallops; flash under the grill just long enough for the cheese to melt, but not so long that it browns. Sprinkle a little cayenne over the top and serve at once.

Scallops Sautéed with Tomato and Garlic

30 g / 1 oz butter
115 g / 4 oz shallots, diced
1 teaspoon soft brown sugar
1 teaspoon tomato purée
450 g / 1 lb tomatoes, skinned,
 seeded and chopped
salt, pepper
12 scallops
2 tablespoons olive oil
2 tablespoons dried breadcrumbs
2 cloves garlic, crushed
1 tablespoon chopped chervil and
 fennel leaves

Melt the butter in a pan and sweat the shallots until transparent. Add brown sugar and tomato purée. Cook 1 minute then add the tomatoes. Stew gently until the tomatoes start to mush. Season and reserve.

Shell and clean the scallops. Heat the olive oil. When it starts to smoke sauté the scallops rapidly, about 3 minutes. Add the breadcrumbs and garlic to the pan. Shake it back and forth so that the crumbs start to crisp and adhere to the scallops.

Arrange the sautéed scallops over the tomato coulis on four plates. Season and sprinkle with chervil and fennel.

Soups

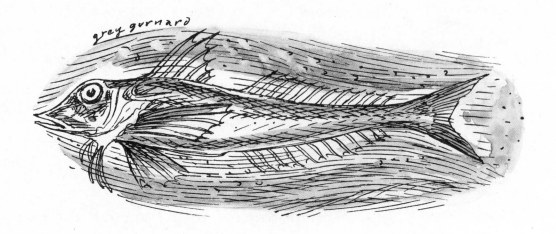

grey gurnard

In the 17th century 'Le Potage' was a substantial dish of meat or fish with vegetables. After going out of fashion, it became such as we know it today, either clear or thickened. Opening a meal, it must be in perfect harmony with the menu as a whole.

Vladimir Durussel in *Etude, Rédaction & Planification des Menus*,
a textbook of the Ecole Hotelière, Lausanne

*L*e *Guide Culinaire* by Escoffier is the chef's Bible. It contains over 400 recipes for soups and their garnishes. These divide into two groups: clear soups (consommés) and thickened soups (purées, crèmes, veloutés). The chapter includes some Provençal soups, international soups (borsch, cock-a-leekie, clam chowder) and some special vegetable soups. Those who nod wisely and tell you that Auguste Escoffier's rigorous recipes are stereotyped have not bothered to read him. His fish soups alone reflect a culinary lore which might have disappeared had he not taken pains to record it. Did professional cooks during the Belle Epoque really make fish bouillon with pike, carp and tench? Did they ever clarify a consommé by mixing caviar with minced pike and whiting? The emotions aroused by rummaging through his guide can be akin to the pleasure a child experiences when he discovers a trunk full of old clothes in an attic. But there is a sense of frustration too. For all the many delightful and surprising variations, Escoffier provides a very limited number of themes. Worse, he advances them as immutable laws.

Rules may be valuable, even essential to a disciplined kitchen brigade, but they ought never to obtrude upon the unfettered alchemy of a cook in his own home. Here making soup is neither a chore nor a science which appoints just so much cream and just so much stock to a given quantity of purée. Soup is a game you can eat. You can concoct suave limpid brews which would charm a Master of the Tea Ceremony or fill a tureen with a steaming aromatic pond of multi-coloured fish which would slake the appetite of a half-starved Breton trawler-man. The art lies in cooking for the occasion. There is no such thing as a proper portion or a correct consistency. Suppose you are going to make a crab soup, no, not a bisque. Wait until you plan to buy a crab for some other meal. After you have poached it, keep some of the soft meat inside the carapace. Reserve as much of the cooking liquor as you think you will need. Then, to make your soup, sweat some onion in butter, add enough flour to absorb it, the poaching liquor, milk and the crabmeat you have saved. Simmer it, blend it, season it, eat it. If you want to add wine or brandy do so. If you want it pinker put in tomato; spicier, half a chilli. Stir in some cream, decorate with fresh chervil, or if you feel like doing something a bit twee, sprinkle chive flowers all over it. On a hot midsummer day serve it chilled with yoghurt and diced cucumber. Live dangerously!

In this case exact proportions count for little. The end result will almost certainly be good, so long as you take the right first step, which is to scrub the crab before sacrificing it. If it was still muddy on the underside of the shell, all the fancy juggling with four-and-twenty spices will have been in vain.

Making good soup stock requires exactly the same common-sense approach. You do not have to sweat diced onions first or squeeze lemon juice into the stock, or add wine, or chop the bones a certain size, or pop a bouquet garni in the pot, but you can if you like. It may not even help to wash the bones and trimmings first. What matters is that they should be fresh. You can tell by examining the blood vessels on the bones; they must still be pink, not brown or black. The skin should have a sweetish aroma of seaweed. If you happen to have a cod or salmon head for the stockpot, it should be bright-eyed, but discard the gills. Whiting bones make delicate stocks, salmon strong. Sole trimmings are better for sauces. Plaice bones are said to be bitter. Avoid the oily fish, mackerel and herring.

Factories once made glue by boiling up crunched bones; they made stock the same way. The longer you simmer fish stock, the stickier the liquid becomes, the less appetizing its taste. Escoffier allowed a maximum of 30 minutes; 20 will suffice; 450 g / 1 lb of bones and trimmings makes a bit less than 600 ml / 1 pint.

A common kitchen saw runs that soup and stews taste better the second day. That may be so, not always. It depends. If you are more interested in the liquid than the fish, the rest does help the flavours to amalgamate. Otherwise make your soup as you want it to taste, then add the fish whole or in pieces close to the time you intend eating it so that it just cooks through. If lumps and gobbets of fish are left in a broth they taste woolly.

Artichoke and Fresh Prawn Soup

450 g / 1 lb uncooked prawns
salt, pepper
½ lemon
4 globe artichokes
50 g / 2 oz flour
50 g / 2 oz butter
1 onion, chopped
80 ml / 3 fl oz dry white wine
115 ml / 4 fl oz double cream
chervil leaves

Drop the prawns into 1.5 litres / 2½ pints of salted water. Simmer 4 minutes, take out the prawns and reserve the cooking liquid. Squeeze the lemon juice into 1.5 litres / 2½ pints of boiling salted water in another pan. Add the artichokes, small ones rather than the gigantic Breton variety. Simmer 20–25 minutes, then remove the artichokes but reserve the liquid.

Make a sandy roux with flour and butter. Add half of the prawn and half the artichoke liquids. Boil, add the onion and simmer 30 minutes. Top up with extra liquid if the soup seems too thick.

Discard the artichoke leaves and scrape out the hairy choke in the centre (you can serve the leaves with vinaigrette as a cocktail accompaniment). Dice the hearts, peel the prawns and chop up the tails.

Add wine to the soup and bring it to the boil. Stir in the cream. Add pepper to taste. Away from the heat stir in the artichoke, prawns and chervil leaves.

Conger and Mussel Soup

1 conger head
1.25 litres / 2 pints mussels
700 g / 1½ lb conger, cut from
    the head end
1 onion, diced
2 tablespoons olive oil
1 teaspoon *herbes de Provence*
2 beef tomatoes, chopped
1 sachet saffron
salt, pepper
parsley, chopped
50 g / 2 oz grated Cheddar

Conger is one of the firmest textured fish you can buy and may take up to half an hour's simmering. It has a better flavour than cod too. Its major drawback is the bones. At the tail end from the stomach backwards are many nasty bones which can put off the most determined piscophile. Even the middle-cut has its share. Conger soup with marigold petals is a Jersey speciality. This is something more gutsy.

Put the head in 1.25 litres / 2 pints of water, simmer 20 minutes and strain the broth. Put the mussels on a tray and pop them into a very hot oven for a couple of minutes, then shell.

Skin the conger and remove the elastic undercoat around it. This cartilaginous tissue would make the conger flesh shrink and toughen. Cube the meat. Fry the onion in oil. Add the *herbes de Provence* and tomatoes. Pour over the stock and simmer 30 minutes. Liquidize the soup and add the saffron dissolved in boiling water.

24

Pour the soup back into the pan and add the conger. Simmer until tender. Check the seasoning and add the mussels. Sprinkle plenty of parsley over the soup and serve the cheese as a garnish.

If you are conscientious, you can pull out the bones with tweezers after sautéing the conger.

Crab Soup with Leek and Monkfish

40 g / 1½ oz butter
40 g / 1½ oz flour
2 shallots, diced
1 teaspoon tomato purée
600 ml / 1 pint crab stock (page 74)
150 ml / ¼ pint milk
115 g / 4 oz brown crabmeat
115 g / 4 oz leeks, finely sliced
50 ml / 2 fl oz medium dry sherry
80 ml / 3 fl oz double cream
1 tablespoon cognac
salt, pepper
350 g / 12 oz monkfish

Make a sandy textured roux with the butter and flour. Add the shallots and tomato purée. Cook 2 minutes more over a low heat, stirring. Add the crab stock, milk and the soft, brown crabmeat. Simmer 20 minutes and add the leeks, and sherry. Simmer another 15 minutes and stir in the cream and cognac. Check the seasoning. Cube the monkfish, add it to the soup and let it cook just long enough to turn opaque.

Lemon Soup with Skate and Broad Beans

chicken feet (about a dozen)
450 g / 1 lb chicken bones, necks, giblets
1 onion
175 g / 6 oz shelled broad beans
450 g / 1 lb skate
15 g / ½ oz butter
2 egg yolks
juice of 1 lemon
salt, pepper
savory, chopped

The Chinese happily cook fish in chicken broth, so why shouldn't we? You need to have chicken feet to make a really good broth. Trim the claws off the feet, blanch them and scrape off the scales. Put them in a pan with bones, necks and giblets. Cover with 1.5 litres / 2½ pints of water. Add the onion, boil, skim and simmer 2 hours. Strain the broth and reduce it to 600 ml / 1 pint. Keep it hot.

Boil the beans for 5 minutes. Squeeze them out of their leathery husks one at a time. Wrap the skate in buttered foil and bake it 20 minutes in a hot oven, 220°C, 425°F, gas mark 7. Ease the meat off the cartilaginous bones.

Whisk the yolks and lemon juice together in a soup tureen. Add the chicken broth, beating all the time. Check the seasoning. Stir in the beans and skate and garnish with savory.

Gurnard Goulash Soup

1 large gurnard
40 g / 1½ oz butter
150 g / 5 oz finely diced onion
60 g / 2 oz finely diced carrot
1 teaspoon sweet paprika
1 tablespoon tomato purée
½ teaspoon caraway seeds
150 ml / ¼ pint dry white wine
1 strip orange zest
salt, pepper
60 g / 2 oz diced capsicum
150 g / 5 oz peeled, cubed waxy
    potatoes
115 g / 4 oz cooked beetroot
150 ml / ¼ pint sour cream

There are several different sorts of gurnard, varying in colour from red to grey. Any will do, but be careful of the spiny fins when handling them.

Fillet the fish, put the head and bones in a pan, cover with 600 ml / 1 pint of water and simmer 20 minutes. Strain the stock.
    Heat the butter in a fresh pan. Stew the onion and carrot with the paprika. Add the tomato purée and caraway seeds. Cook over a low heat for 2 minutes, then pour over three-quarters of the stock. Add wine and simmer 15 minutes. Add the orange zest. Adjust the seasoning. Add capsicum and potato. Cook 20 minutes. Dice the gurnard flesh and stir into the soup together with the beetroot. Heat through. Serve with sour cream.

Garlic and Fish Soup

For the rouille:
1 red chilli, deseeded
½ red capsicum
1 clove garlic
1 egg
250 ml / 9 fl oz groundnut oil
250 ml / 9 fl oz olive oil

For the soup:
1 French loaf (*baguette*, or better,
    a *ficelle*)
40 g / 1½ oz butter
1 head garlic
300 ml / ½ pint chicken stock
300 ml / ½ pint milk
450 g / 1 lb white fish
salt, pepper

Rouille, the marseillaise accompaniment to bouillabaisse, can be pungent or mild. This is a milder version.

Purée the chilli, capsicum and garlic in a food processor. Add the egg and whizz up the mixture. Blend in the oils to make a thick sauce and season. You will only need half of this sauce. (The rest will keep for about three days, but not in the fridge or it will separate.)
    Slice the loaf and dry it out in a low oven. Melt the butter in a pan. Peel the garlic and stew the cloves over a low flame till they become soft (this may take 30 minutes). Add the stock and milk. Simmer 20 minutes then blend the soup with a tablespoon of rouille. Season. Return to the pan and over the lowest possible heat and add the white fish cut in smallish pieces. Simmer 2 minutes. Fork through the soup to flake the fish. Serve the soup in bowls with bread and rouille offered separately.
    For a change, try adding a hint of lime juice or lime vinegar to the rouille. It's not classical, but pretty good.

Onion Soup with Red Bream

450 g / 1 lb onions
30 g / 1 oz flour
50 g / 2 oz butter
½ clove garlic, crushed
sea salt
700 ml / 1¼ pints chicken stock
150 ml / ¼ pint dry white wine
450 g / 1 lb fillet red bream
pepper

Red bream is often sold as rock salmon and is less exciting than the black bream which is occasionally caught along the south coast. Even so, when fresh it makes good eating.

Slice the onions into rings and dredge a little flour over them. Melt the butter in a pan and add the onion. Cook slowly until soft and golden. Add the garlic and salt. Pour on the chicken stock and wine. Simmer 45 minutes then reduce over a high heat to about 600 ml / 1 pint. Check the seasoning.

Cut the bream into pieces about 5 cm / 2 inches long and drop them in the soup. Cover the pan and let the fish cook in the soup off the heat; serve.

Seatrout and Lobster Soup

70 g / 2½ oz butter
1 tablespoon groundnut oil
115 g / 4 oz carrot, diced
150 g / 5 oz onion, diced
1 shallot, finely chopped
1 clove garlic, crushed
½ bayleaf
1 pinch thyme
3 tomatoes, skinned and chopped
300 ml / 1 pint lobster stock
300 ml / ½ pint Riesling
30 g / 1 oz flour
30 g / 1 oz tomato purée
80 ml / 3 fl oz double cream
salt, pepper
4 tablespoons chopped fennel
   bulb
150 g / 5 oz poached or steamed
   seatrout, flaked
1 tablespoon fennel leaves,
   chopped

Heat 40 g / 1½ oz butter and the oil in a pan. Add carrot, onion and shallot. Stew over a low heat until the onion becomes transparent. Add the garlic, bayleaf and thyme. Cook for a minute or so, then add the tomatoes, stock and the Riesling. Simmer 30 minutes. In another pan make a light roux with the remaining butter and the flour. Add the tomato purée and cook for 2 minutes. Strain the hot lobster-flavoured broth on to the roux. Simmer 30 minutes more. Stir in the cream. Check the seasoning.

To serve, stir in the fennel and seatrout together with any scraps of lobster salvaged from another dish. Garnish with fennel leaves.

NOTE: this is already a rich soup, but you can enrich it further with a shot of high cholesterol lobster butter (page 38).

Seatrout Souchie

450 g / 1 lb seatrout trimmings
  (head, skin, bones)
150 ml / ¼ pint Muscadet
80 g / 3 oz parsley stalks
200 g / 7 oz chopped leeks
4 × 150 g / 5 oz seatrout fillets
8 tablespoons chopped parsley
115 g / 4 oz finely shredded
  sorrel
sea salt, pepper

Put the seatrout trimmings in a pan with 450 ml / ¾ pint of water, the muscadet, parsley stalks and leeks. Simmer 20 minutes and strain the liquid into a fresh pan.

Put the seatrout fillets into the boiling, strained stock and take the pan off the heat straightaway. Leave to stand 7 minutes.

Mix the parsley and sorrel with 350 ml / 12 fl oz of the stock. Season. Pour into four old-fashioned soup bowls with wide rims. Arrange the fillets on top and sprinkle a few grains of salt over them.

Red Lentil and Flaked Crab Soup

Serves 6–8
2 bayleaves
1 onion
2 cloves
1 carrot, chopped
150 g / 5 oz red lentils
1 teaspoon turmeric
1 dried chilli
300 ml / ½ pint crab stock (page
  74)
1 tablespoon lime juice
salt, pepper
350 g / 12 oz flaked white
  crabmeat

Fasten the bayleaves to an onion with two cloves. Put them in a pan with carrot and lentils, a scant teaspoon of turmeric and the chilli. Cover with 1.5 litres / 2½ pints of water and the crab stock. Boil, skim and simmer 90 minutes. Discard the onion, bayleaves and cloves. Blend the soup in a liquidizer. Stir in the lime juice and check the seasoning. Pour the soup into four bowls and sprinkle with flaked crabmeat.

Shellfish Soup with Quenelles

uncooked seatrout mousseline
  (page 89)
50 g / 2 oz unsalted butter
115 g / 4 oz white of leek
salt, pepper
18 mussels
6 scallops
6 prawns
80 g / 3 oz white crabmeat

Quenelle and mousseline mixtures freeze well uncooked, but you must defrost them thoroughly in the fridge before cooking. For this recipe you will need only a small proportion of the seatrout mousseline, so the surplus can be frozen.

Prepare two sheets of baking parchment, a bowl of hot water and two coffee spoons. Dipping the spoons in the hot water for each quenelle, mould baby quenelles which look like sugared almonds. Make 24 and freeze

30 g / 1 oz dried Jew's ear
  mushrooms (soaked for ½
  hour
900 ml / 1½ pints fish stock
  (page 23)
2.5 cm / 1 inch fresh ginger root

the remaining mixture.

Melt the butter in a saucepan, add the shredded leek and salt. Cover and stew 5 minutes over a low heat. Open the mussels by leaving them in a hot oven for about 5 minutes. Shell them and nip off their beards. Thinly slice the scallops. Shell the prawns, split them and remove the intestines. Flake the crabmeat. Cut the mushrooms into strips. Pour the fish stock over the leeks. Add mushrooms and ginger, cut into threads. Simmer 5 minutes. Add the quenelles and simmer 2 minutes. Add prawns and simmer 2 minutes. Add mussels and scallops. Simmer 3 minutes. Stir in the crab, check the seasoning and serve.

Smoked Fish and Vinegar Soup

220 g / 8 oz cubed potatoes
80 g / 3 oz diced onions
80 g / 3 oz sliced mushrooms
2 tablespoons groundnut oil
1 × 400 g / 14 oz can of
  tomatoes
1 smoked mackerel
600 ml / 1 pint fish stock
  (page 23)
1 tablespoon *vieux vinaigre de vin*
salt, pepper
3 spring onions, finely sliced

Stew the vegetables in the oil until they colour. Add the tomatoes and the flesh of half the smoked mackerel. Add the stock. Boil 20 minutes and add the rest of the mackerel and the vinegar. Adjust the seasoning. Stir the spring onions into the soup and serve.

Plaice, Spinach and Watercress Soup

220 g / 8 oz plaice fillets
30 g / 1 oz butter
50 g / 2 oz smoked mackerel
  fillet
2 shallots, diced
30 g / 1 oz patna rice
115 g / 4 oz spinach
½ bunch watercress
80 ml / 3 fl oz double cream
salt, pepper
2 tablespoons flour
oil for frying

Stew half the plaice for 2 minutes in melted butter, then add the flaked mackerel, shallots and rice. Cook until the rice is well coloured with butter then pour over 600 ml / 1 pint of water. Simmer 10 minutes and add the spinach and watercress. Simmer 10 more minutes and season. Cool slightly then liquidize the soup. Return to the pan and stir in the cream. Check the seasoning.

Cut the rest of the plaice into strips, roll them in flour and fry them in oil for 2 minutes, then drain on absorbent paper and use them to garnish the soup.

Whiting and Monkfish Soup

700 g / 1½ lb whiting
1 beef tomato
2 tablespoons olive oil
50 g / 2 oz diced onion
50 g / 2 oz diced shallots
50 g / 2 oz diced celeriac
2 cloves garlic, crushed
sea salt, pepper
300 ml / ½ pint dry white wine
1 sachet saffron
115 g / 4 oz monkfish
1 tablespoon chopped fennel,
   thyme and chives

Fillet and skin the whiting. Put the skin, head and bones in a pan with 450 ml / ¾ pint of water. Bring to the boil, skim and simmer 20 minutes. Strain the stock.

Drop the tomato in boiling water 12 seconds, skin, seed and chop the flesh. Heat the olive oil. Sweat the onion, shallots and celeriac until they start to soften. Add the tomato and garlic with a little salt. Add the stock and white wine. Bring to the boil, then simmer 1 hour. Dissolve the saffron in a little boiling water and stir into the soup. Cut the monkfish into small cubes and cut the whiting into strips. Add the fish to the soup. Stir in the herbs, check the seasoning and serve.

Whiting and Sweetcorn Chowder

115 g / 4 oz onions
220 g / 8 oz potatoes
115 g / 4 oz leeks
½ clove garlic
115 g / 4 oz bacon, rind removed
80 g / 3 oz butter
900 ml / 1½ pints milk
salt, pepper
450 g / 1 lb whiting
200 g/ 7 oz cooked sweetcorn
   kernels
1 tablespoon chopped parsley
2 tablespoons double cream
   (optional)

This is a cross between the stand-by leek and potato soup and an American chowder.

Dice the onions; cube the potatoes; chop the leeks so they are roughly the size of your little fingernail. Crush the garlic and dice the bacon.

Melt the butter in a large pan and add the above ingredients. Let them stew over a low flame for about 5 minutes. Add the milk and bring it to simmering point. Season and continue simmering till the vegetables are tender. Chop the skinned whiting into pieces roughly 2.5cm 1 inch across. Add them to the pan away from the heat together with the sweetcorn kernels. Stir in the parsley and some cream if you like. Grind plenty of pepper over the top and let the soup stand 3–4 minutes before serving.

Cocks, Hens, Spiders and Cockroaches

spider crab

But whilst the fish is displayed dead, the crustacean stalls are a writhing mass of life; crabs, spider crabs, scampi, crawfish, lobsters, everything moves, palpitates, quivers and in this century of sterile food, it is reassuring to see that it is still possible to find live food.

From a description of a fish market in *La Cuisine Bretonne*
by Eliane Roussel-Le Sciellour

Vegetarians always fire the same broadside at carnivores: 'If you want to eat steak,' they argue, 'you should be prepared to kill the cow.' For shellfish eating, the theory turns into practice if you intend to do the cooking. When you buy a lobster you do not buy a dead fish, but a live one.

Cooks of previous generations were never over-squeamish. They popped a crab into boiling water or split a lobster down the middle without a second thought. Then, about 50 years ago, morality donned an apron and entered the kitchen. The RSPCA advised that it was kinder to put a crustacean alive into a pot of cold water and bring it slowly to the boil. The slow temperature rise numbed the nervous system and the creature met its end painlessly. Fashions, even in kindness, change and for lobsters, at least, a plunge into a boiling bath is now supposedly a swifter and more humane end.

When a crustacean dies before it leaves the fishmonger, the edible parts decompose much faster than with other fishes. Even if there were no risk of food poisoning, you would need to cook it from live because otherwise the flavour loses its sweetness, the texture turns cotton-woolly and the odour is putrescent, as anyone who has come across a crab decaying on a beach will know.

You will not find live crustaceans in many fish shops along the southwest coast. Devon is not Brittany. The crabs are pre-cooked during the summer for the rash of holidaymakers who are more curious than discerning. The crabs are hosed down to wash off superficial sand and mud and piled willy-nilly into a marmite of seawater which is brought to the boil. They simmer for about 20 minutes, long enough to make them easy to pick. Most are overcooked and dry. One Lyme crab-fisherman insists that his customers like them that way. A little more care is given to lobsters, but only because they are a more valuable catch and in scant supply.

Whenever a wharfside conversation turns to lobsters and crabs, sex rears its head. There are partisans of the 'cocks', the males, and those who favour the females, the 'hens'.

It's not easy to tell the sex of a lobster. The hen is often broader in the beam. The cock has two sharp swimmerets at the top of the tail, nearest the body. Obviously, only the hens carry 'berries', the eggs. Size is a more important guide to how well a lobster will eat. The smallest ones, sometimes called cockroaches, are the sweetest and most tender. Large lobsters and crawfish weighing over a couple of pounds start to become chewy and dry. Condition also matters. Tickle a lobster in the middle of its tail fins and it should start to buck convulsively. If it fails to react, it may have been out of its natural element for too long. The shell should also be hard. Lobsters moult once a year and are out of condition soon after fitting their new armour plating.

With both spider crabs and shankers, picking the 'chaps' from the 'gels' is much easier. Turned on to their backs, the ladies display a triangular stomacher or panel with a hairy rim covering the underbelly. There may be little scientific evidence to support this assertion, but hen crabs seem to be smaller and more tasty. Their carapace often has more of the cream, the soft meat. They lie more heavily in the hand. Cocks, however, both crabs and lobsters, have larger claws. Lobsters are fighters. Leave them in a tank without shackling their claws in elastic bands and they will cripple each other. Those missing a claw are actually called cripples and sell for half the price of perfect specimens. Of the two claws one is better at cutting and the other at crunching. To pick up a lobster, grasp it firmly on top of the body behind the eyes.

The big difference between the rough shelled spider crabs and the cumbersome shankers is that spiders do not have large pincers. That may also explain why West Countrymen turn up their noses at them. Locally, they are unsaleable, but the fishermen have a lucrative market. They keep them in a net a few yards off the shore and when they have filled the net they sell them for export to Spain. There is no dearth of spiders. Shanker crabs are still plentiful, but lobsters have been sadly overfished. Crawfish or rock lobsters are a rarity. Except at Dartmouth, it is rare to see anything but a frozen prawn in the shops. In Mrs Beeton's days, shellfish and crustaceans were prolific along the west coast. Today the osier pots are often no more than a decoration lying on the beach.

Crab

Before cooking a live crab, turn it on its back and scrub its tummy. A rough muddy film accumulates on the underside of the carapace which will make the precious stock musty if you don't wash it away.

Choose a cock crab if you want to have a more substantial amount of the white meat, and a hen if you want more of the brown meat which lodges inside the shell.

Roy, my crab supplier, will always pick me a 'lively' crab, one that would damage your big toe given half a chance. It should be heavy in the hand, a good sign that there will be plenty of meat in the carapace.

On the Devon coast, the accepted opinion is that you put a live crab into cold water and bring it to the boil to cook it, whereas you drop a lobster into boiling water. Seawater is better, but you can add a tablespoon of sea salt for every 2 litres / 3 pints of tap water.

Drop the crab into cold salted water. Immerse it fully. Cover the pan and bring the water to the boil. Take it off the heat and let the crab cool in its poaching liquid for at least 30 minutes. This method seems to work with crabs of all sizes.

Picking a crab is time-consuming, but not difficult if you raid the family tool box. A mole-spanner will crack the claws of crabs weighing up to 2 kilos / 4 pounds. A meat skewer will poke the meat out of the body. The only inedible parts are the stomach (located behind the eyes) and the gills or witch's fingers.

Crabmeat with Chilli Oil Dressing

1 tablespoon white wine vinegar
2 teaspoons Dijon mustard
3 tablespoons chilli oil
1 tablespoon chopped shallots
450 g / 1 lb white crabmeat
salt, pepper

You can buy chilli oil from oriental foodstores, but you can also make it at home (page 57).

Beat the vinegar, mustard and oil together. Mix in the shallots and crab. Season. Chill and serve with an endive (chicory) salad or with avocado.

Crab, Bacon and Celeriac

½ lemon
220 g / 8 oz cubed celeriac
salt
220 g / 8 oz green streaky bacon,
   rind removed
40 g / 1½ oz butter
220 g / 8 oz white crabmeat
220 g / 8 oz soft crabmeat
   (brown or cream)
cayenne pepper

Squeeze a dash of lemon juice into a pan of boiling salted water. Simmer the celeriac in the water until tender. Drain. Cut the bacon into thin lardons, i.e. across the grain into strips about twice the thickness of matchsticks. Sauté them in butter. When they start to colour, add the celeriac. Continue cooking until the bacon turns golden, then stir in the crabmeat. Heat through, sprinkle cayenne on the mixture and squeeze some lemon juice on top.

Spoon the mixture into a clean crab shell and serve hot.

Crab Salad and Toasted Pine Kernels

50 g / 2 oz pine kernels
salt, pepper
115 g / 4 oz spinach
220 g / 8 oz new potatoes
1 teaspoon English mustard
1 diced shallot
1 tablespoon wine vinegar
3 tablespoons groundnut oil
220 g / 8 oz crabmeat

Gently roast the pine kernels in a frying pan over a low heat. When coloured turn them on to a plate and salt them.

Blanch the spinach in boiling salted water for a few seconds, drain and pat dry. Cut the potatoes in small pieces and boil in salted water until tender.

Make a dressing with mustard, shallot, vinegar, oil and seasoning. (Try adding pine kernel oil instead of the groundnut oil if you can find it in the shops.)

Arrange a little spinach on four plates. Dab with dressing. Pile the warm potatoes on them and coat with dressing. Combine the rest of the dressing with the crabmeat. Pile the crab on to the potato and fork through it until it looks fluffy. Sprinkle pine kernels on top.

Scrambled Egg and Crab

Drop a couple of handfuls of small sea beet leaves into boiling, salted water, simmer 5 minutes and drain. Melt 50 g / 2 oz butter in a large frying pan. Add 50 g / 2 oz of diced onion and sweat over a low flame until transparent.

Whisk 4–5 eggs and season. Pour them into the frying pan and cook over a very low flame until soft

34

curds start to form. Continue to cook the eggs, stirring them until they become creamy, then fold in 115 g / 4 oz of white crabmeat, the onion and the sea beet leaves. Beat in a spoonful of cream to stop the eggs overcooking.

Serve on hot buttered toast.

Gratin of Lemon Sole and Crab

1 hen crab weighing about
   450 g / 1 lb
salt, cayenne pepper
8 lemon sole fillets, skinned
15 g / ½ oz butter
2 egg yolks
150 ml / ¼ pint double cream
1 teaspoon lemon juice

Put the crab in cold salted water, bring it to the boil and let it cool in its own cooking liquid. Reserve the liquid and pick the crab, keeping the white and dark meats separate.

Fold the lemon sole fillets around the flaked white meat. Lay two fillets each in four single-portion buttered gratin dishes. Pour 3 tablespoons of the crab's cooking liquid over each portion. Cover with buttered greaseproof paper and bake in a hot oven, 220°C, 425°F, gas mark 7, for 7 minutes. While the fish is cooking switch on the grill so that it becomes very hot. Whisk the yolks, cream, lemon juice and a pinch of salt until the mixture starts to thicken.

Strain the liquor in the gratin dishes into a blender and liquidize with the dark crabmeat. Fold this into the yolks and cream. Add a pinch of cayenne. Spoon the sauce over the rolled fillets. Glaze the sauce under the grill until it turns brown—not black, and serve.

Crab Soufflés

30 g / 1 oz flour
40 g / 1½ oz butter
150 ml / ¼ pint milk
salt, pepper
2 eggs, separated
1 tablespoon medium sherry
175 g / 6 oz crabmeat

The underside of a crab shell has an inner rim which you can easily snap away with a well-aimed hammer blow. Prepare 4 carapaces in this way; they should come from crabs weighing about 450–700 g / 1–1½ lb. You can re-use these shells providing that you scrub and sterilize them after each use.

Make a sandy roux with the butter and flour. Beat in the milk and bring to the boil. Whisk and simmer 10 minutes. Season. Off the heat beat the egg yolks into the mixture, taking care not to turn them into scrambled eggs, and the sherry. Fold the crabmeat into the sauce.

Preheat the oven to 200°C, 400°F, gas mark 6 then

whisk the egg whites until stiff, but not crumbly. Fold them into the crab and sauce base. Butter the insides of the crab shells. Fill them almost to the rim with the mixture and bake for approximately 10–12 minutes until the filling is well risen and a mid-brown colour.

The soufflés should be nearly cooked through with just a hint of moistness in the centre.

Sautéed Crab Claws with Bacon and Courgette Ribbons

4 large cooked crab claws
50 g / 2 oz butter
220 g / 8 oz smoked streaky
  bacon, rind removed
1 clove garlic, finely chopped
sea salt, pepper
450 g / 1 lb courgettes (green
  and yellow if possible)
few oyster mushrooms (optional)

Pick the meat from the crab claws. You should have about 500 g / 18 oz crabmeat. Melt half the butter in a pan; dice the bacon, fry it for 2 minutes. Add the garlic and cook for a minute. Add crabmeat and cook until it heats through.

Season with sea salt and plenty of ground pepper.

Slice the courgettes into ribbons with a potato peeler, drop them in boiling salted water for a couple of minutes and drain. Toss them in the remaining melted butter and arrange them on four dinner plates. Spoon the hot crab and bacon on top.

A few chopped oyster mushrooms cooked with the bacon before the crabmeat goes into the pan is a good addition.

Spider Crab Pen'March

½ cucumber
1 cooked spider crab weighing
  about 1 kg / 2¼ lbs
100 ml / 3–4 fl oz mayonnaise
25 g / 1 oz red capsicum, finely
  diced
3 mint leaves, finely shredded
1 bird's eye chilli, seeded and
  diced as finely as possible

Have you ever suspected that cookery writers spend their lives filching other writers' recipes? This is a short insight into how some of us work, some of the time. About a dozen years ago, I came across Crabe Pen'March in a magazine called *Femmes d'Aujourd'hui*. It sounded evocative and vaguely Breton, so I adapted it as a starter for a book on bistro cooking. Since then I've played with it some more and the following version has emerged . . .

Peel, seed, cube and salt the cucumber 30 minutes. Rinse and pat dry.

Pick the white meat from the crab and reserve. Use the brown meat for another recipe. Combine the crabmeat with mayonnaise, capsicum, mint, chilli and cucumber. Wash out the spider crab's carapace and fill it with the mixture.

Lobster

The sweetest and most tender lobsters weigh less than a pound. There are alternative ways of boiling them. Either plunge them *head first* into boiling salted water or a shellfish stock, and simmer them for 15–20 minutes, depending on their size, or put them in a pan of cold stock or water, enough to cover, bring it to the boil, simmer 12–15 minutes, then remove the lobster from the pan when it has turned a bright red. The process in either case is like boiling a large egg.

You can split a whole lobster with a heavy kitchen knife, but it is neater done with a pair of poultry shears (or garden shears, providing they are clean and sharp!).

Snip off the tail fins.

Clip through the shell lengthwise from the tail, to a point between the eyes.

Turn the lobster over on to its back and clip parallel to the first line.

Split the lobster in half, preferably with a stainless steel knife, using the sectioned shell as a guide.

Take out the stomach, which is behind the eyes and the gills.

Remove the intestine which runs the length of the tail.

Crack the claws.

The following advice for dealing with lobster claws in a restaurant is given by Almeric Fish in *Lazometrics*:

1 Take the claw in both hands, place the tips of the thumbs together at its mid-point.
2 With a sharp, snapping motion, break the claw cleanly in two.

If the claw refuses to snap after the third or fourth attempt:

1 Lay it surreptitiously but with firm muscle action under the table on a clean napkin.
2 Stamp on it.

Baked Lobster

This is better done with a medium sized lobster weighing at least 600 g / 1¼ lb. Use a sharp and heavy kitchen knife with a good point on it, a professional's knife.

Lay the lobster flat, stomach down on a chopping board. Hold the lobster steady and rest the point of the knife just behind the eyes. Plunge it down firmly and take it out again. Turn the fish around and cut off the tail fins. Split it and when you have the two halves scoop out the stomach sac behind the eyes. Take out the intestine which runs along the tail.

Lay the two halves side by side in a baking tin with the raw meat uppermost. Season.

Bake the lobster in a very hot oven, 240°C, 475°F, gas mark 9, allowing 10 minutes per inch of thickness (a trick of the late James Beard, the Dean of American cookery).

Mash up 2 tablespoons of the best butter you can buy with a teaspoon of chopped fresh tarragon, a teaspoon of diced shallots, a teaspoon of chopped parsley and a small pinch of salt. When the lobster has cooked, break and crack the claws. Take out the tail meat from its shell. Spread some of the herb butter in the shell and replace the meat on top. Spread the rest of the butter on top.

Lobster Milk and Lobster Butter

The price of shellfish being what it is, it seems criminal to waste any of the flavour contained in the nooks and crannies of lobster, crawfish and prawns.

Lobster eggs and the coral which forms a vermilion strip inside the carapace can both be used as garnishes or for sauces.

The shell of cooked lobster or crawfish can supply the basis of sauces or stocks.

Start by pounding the shells in a mortar. You can use a food processor, but only if the shellfish is small and the processor powerful. Once it is well broken up add 220 g / 8 oz of unsalted butter per 450 g / 1 lb of shells. Continue mashing or blending. Scrape the paste from the mortar or bowl into a pan and heat gently until the butter starts to foam. Pour over 600 ml / 1 pint of milk. Bring to the boil. Simmer 2 minutes. Take the pan off the heat and leave to stand for 5 minutes. Strain the liquid through a fine sieve into a bowl and leave it to get cold. The lobster or shellfish butter will set on top of the shellfish milk.

Cut the butter into small cubes and freeze for up to 4 months. Serve with plain grilled or poached fish or to enhance soups such as Seatrout and Lobster Soup (page 27).

You can make a simple old-fashioned sauce with the milk. Melt 50 g / 2 oz ordinary butter in a pan. Add 50 g / 1½ oz flour. Make a roux. Add 600 ml / 1 pint of the shellfish-flavoured milk and bring it to the boil, whisking throughout to prevent lumps. Simmer 20 minutes over the lowest possible heat. Beat in a knob of the shellfish butter. Add 150 ml / ¼ pint of cream. Check the seasoning. Add a little sherry just before serving.

A combination of the broth in which you boil a lobster, the milk and the butter makes a good soup too.

Grilled Lobster with Sherry

40 g / 1½ oz butter
1 pinch hot paprika
1 × 700 g / 1½ lb lobster
1 shallot, diced
50 ml / 2 fl oz fish stock
50 ml / 2 fl oz manzanilla sherry
150 ml / ¼ pint double cream
salt, pepper

Melt half the butter in a small pan and add the paprika. Let it cook slowly for 2 minutes so the spice loses its rawness. Split the lobster. Scoop out the stomach sac between the eyes and pull out the intestine. Put the two halves shell-side down in a shallow baking tin. Brush the raw meat with the paprika butter. Grill the lobster 15 minutes, brushing it with paprika butter at intervals.

In another pan, stew the shallot in the rest of the butter. Deglaze with stock and sherry. Let the liquid reduce to a syrupy consistency. Stir in the cream and reduce to a coating consistency.

Taste the sauce and add more sherry if you like. Adjust the seasoning.

Pour a tablespoon of sherry sauce over each lobster half and serve the remainder of the sauce separately.

Cockroach Salad

For the sorbet:

220 g / 8 oz tomatoes, peeled
  and chopped
½ eating apple (Cox's), chopped
1 teaspoon diced shallot
1 tablespoon dry white wine
salt, cayenne pepper, pepper
lemon juice to taste
6 basil leaves

4–6 'cockroaches' (small lobsters)
1 tablespoon vinegar
½ teaspoon mustard
2 tablespoons oil
1 heaped tablespoon clotted
  cream
salt
115 g / 4 oz each celery, carrot
  and bulb fennel

Cockroach is the nickname for baby lobsters. The smallest catchable size is limited by law, but lobsters 25 cm / 10 inches from eye to tail can be eaten without fear of prosecution. One this size will cook in 5 minutes dropped into boiling water. Allow one per person.

To make the sorbet, put the tomatoes, apple, shallot, wine, salt and black pepper in a pan and cook until the mixture has reduced and started to thicken. Add lemon juice, basil and a hint of cayenne. Liquidize and then put the mixture in an ice cream machine to freeze.

Boil the 'cockroaches', halve them and take out the stomach sacs. Make a dressing with vinegar, mustard, oil, cream and salt. Spoon over the cooled lobster. Cut the celery, carrot and fennel into thin slices. Arrange them on plates with the lobster. Place a scoop of tomato sorbet on to each plate (you will have some left over) and serve without delay.

Real Food for Real Fish

It has come to be a world of burgers and quick-fried chicken.

The Fast-Food Guide by Michael Jacobson and Sarah Fritschner

What is *real food*? In what sense is canned tomato soup, for instance, unreal? Where should the junk food line be drawn? The word 'natural' applied to food creates a similar dialectical difficulty. Is the flesh of an orange natural and its zest, sprayed with preservative diphenyl, unnatural? Has farmed salmon or trout been denatured?

There is no pat answer. Pointing an accusing finger at the processed food or agrochemical industries or food technologists or plant geneticists (the list of indicted groups and bodies could be extended) pays no dividends. The whole additive issue has been raised from a factual to an emotional plane. Food polemics often disguise the bitter flavour of real politics.

The frontier between *real food* and everything else zigzags in 20 different directions. Much of the ground on either side is contested. Raw food, occurring in nature, untampered with by man, may be beyond reproach; fruit, vegetables, meat from domesticated animals or fish, dairy produce, cereals all lie across the imaginary border.

Hydroponic tomatoes, frozen peas, battery eggs, pasteurized cheese serve the ends of producer and consumer. They have evolved because millions of us want to buy them, and because few people are so obsessive about what they eat that

41

they treat each meal as an intense aesthetic or religious experience.

What is dangerous in the 20th-century food of the rich nations is that the tide of mass production should so engulf us that at one end of the food chain nobody bothers to gather, grow or hunt for *real foods* and that at the other end nobody would appreciate or recognize them even if they were available.

Real food, accepting that there is such a thing, does not bear a factory imprint. Its quality is not guaranteed. It can furnish unpleasant as well as exalting surprises. Cut open a dozen boletus mushrooms growing under a beech hedge and half will be riddled with parasites. Wasps usually discover the best plums before we do.

In the fringe of counties ringing Lyme Bay – Dorset, Devon and Somerset – *real food*, figuratively speaking, does not grow on trees. Anyone can find blackberries in September, but discovering a good Cheddar maker or drinkable cider requires local knowledge. The flood of factory products has all but wiped out traditional farm crafts. Meadows speckled with white mushrooms are few and far between. If you know of one, you keep quiet and treat it as your own private domain. An abundant crop of sloes one year is followed by a dearth the next. Free-range hens stop laying eggs in winter while the boxed-in battery ones stay on the job until the end of their useful working career.

Even someone with an educated palate may not be able to distinguish between a free-range and a battery egg. Nor is that so surprising, since the standardized free-range egg does not exist for comparison. In the kitchen, you can sense a good egg from its extra fluffiness when you whip, whisk or beat. Scrambled eggs set better too; but the clincher is the boiled egg test. Dip a 'soldier' into the yolk; if it drips then the quality is battery. If the yolk clings to the toast the egg passes muster.

There is a simple nuance between pasteurized and unpasteurized Cheddar. At three months old, professional tasters would be hard put to tell them apart. At a year the enzymes – which have been destroyed in the pasteurized cheese – will have developed a palette of subtle tastes in the *live* cheese. Not that un-pasteurized Cheddar automatically wins any head to head contest. Truckles (the small wheels weighing a few pounds) tend to be drier and deader than larger cheeses weighing 60 lb, regardless of how they have been made.

For the fish cook, pasteurization has little impact on the quality of fresh cream. Boiling and reducing it for sauces takes away any special character it may have had. In most cases the cream is a catalyst for other ingredients. But fresh cream, bought at the farm gate, is usually worth having. If it has not been heat-treated it will ripen, thicken, and eventually sour rather than turn bitter. When preparing a sauce, less goes further and gives a more supple, unctuous texture.

Semi-legible signs down country lanes still advertise cider—scrumpy. Real it may be, good it rarely is. Sour, vinegary, mouldy, redolent of metal filings are all descriptions which could be matched to the cloudy brews squeezed from local presses. But there are exceptions, like the clean, balanced ciders made from vintage cider apples such as Kingston Black, Fox Whelp and Morgan Sweet which pour from the vats of Julian Temperley at Burrow Hill.

It is tempting to laud wild foods for their own sake rather than their intrinsic merit. Unless a cook has the patience to persist with an uncommon raw material, he may be disappointed. Shaggy ink cap mushrooms are abundant at the tail end of summer. Drop them in a hot pan and they collapse leaving liquor bubbling in the pan and the elongated caps flabby and unappetizing. On the other hand, they can be converted into a ketchup which will spike a dish of herring roes most effectively. Elderberries, nettles, horseradish, wild garlic, the number of edible plants and fungi run to hundreds. Only a handful are worth cooking with regularly.

Baked Brill with a Clotted Cream Sauce

1 × 1.35 kg / 3 lb brill
115 ml / 4 fl oz dry white wine
  or cider
220 g / 8 oz leek
50 g / 2 oz butter
2 Cox's apples
115 g / 4 oz mushrooms
2 tablespoons cognac or Calvados
350 g / 12 oz clotted cream
salt, pepper

Cut the head and fins off the brill and put them in a pan with wine or cider. Simmer the stock 20 minutes and strain.

Cut the leek into postage stamp-sized pieces. Butter an ovenproof dish large enough for the brill. Spread leeks over the bottom of the dish. Cut the peeled apples into 12 segments each. Put them round the sides of the dish. Lay the brill in the dish black skin downwards, and pour the stock over it. Bake about 15 minutes in a very hot oven, 230°C, 450°F, gas mark 8. Baste the fish a couple of times.

Slice the mushrooms and sauté them in the remaining butter. Heat and flame the Calvados or cognac. Pour it over the cooked fish. Lift out the brill without breaking it and lay it on a serving dish. Strain the liquid into a frying pan and reduce to 150 ml / ¼ pint. Beat in the clotted cream without letting it boil. Adjust the seasoning. Add leek and apple to the sauce together with the sautéed mushrooms. For presentation purposes pour the sauce over the brill, although it is actually easier to serve fish and sauce separately.

43

Gratin of Shellfish and Oyster Mushrooms

175 g / 6 oz oyster mushrooms
50 g / 2 oz butter
16 mussels
1 tablespoon dry white wine
4 scallops, shelled
300 ml / ½ pint double cream
50 g / 2 oz grated Cheddar
1 teaspoon arrowroot
1 tablespoon medium sherry
salt, pepper
115 g / 4 oz shelled prawns

Snip the ends off the oyster mushrooms. Slice them and fry them in butter over a high flame so they colour rapidly (do not let the butter burn). Remove from the pan and reserve. Add the mussels and wine to the pan and place over a high heat until the mussels open. Take the mussels out and reserve. Add the scallops and cook 3 minutes, turning after a minute or two. Take them out of the pan and reserve. Add the cream and reduce it until it starts to thicken. Stir in the Cheddar. Dissolve the arrowroot in the sherry. Whisk it into the sauce to stabilize it. Adjust the seasoning. Remove the mussels from their shells and put them with the scallops, prawns and oyster mushrooms in an ovenproof dish. Pour over the sauce and flash under a hot grill to brown.

John Dory Stew with Buttered Parsnips

1.35 kg / 3 lb John Dory
250 g / 9 oz parsnip
30 g / 1 oz unsalted butter
50 g / 2 oz onion
1 pinch thyme
½ teaspoon caster sugar
salt, pepper
2 tomatoes
½–1 teaspoon chopped wild garlic (optional)

John Dory start swimming into Lyme Bay towards the end of winter. Most are small, weighing only a few ounces. Occasionally you find a whopper of 1½–2 kg / 3–4 lb. Dory produce delicious, gelatinous stock. Coping with Dory requires care, because the fins are spiny and there is a spiky ridge along the back.

Fillet a large Dory (or four small ones). Start from the edge and work to the centre. Skin the fish as you would a sole, but—surprise, surprise!—under the skin you will find three rather than two fillets.

Peel the parsnips (organically grown ones are often tastier), halve them and cut out the woody core. Slice the tender part into thin chips, blanch 5 minutes in boiling salted water and drain.

Melt the butter in a large frying pan, add the diced onion and stew till tender. Add parsnip, fresh thyme and sugar. Turn up the heat and glaze. Season and reduce the heat. Lay the fillets on top and let them steam 5 minutes, turning them at half-time. Blanch, skin, seed and chop the tomatoes. Cook with the fish long enough to heat them through. Grind pepper over the Dory, garnish with wild garlic if you like the taste.

44

John Dory Fillets with a Julienne of Leeks

4 John Dory
1 slice lemon
50 g / 2 oz white of leek
4 shallots, diced
40 g./ 1½ oz butter
250 ml / 9 fl oz dry cider
300 ml / ½ pint double cream
15 g / ½ oz finely chopped red capsicum
salt, pepper

Fillet the Dory (see previous page). Make a stock with skin, bones, lemon slice and 450 ml / ¾ pint of water. Simmer 20 minutes and strain. Cut the leeks in thin matchstick-sized threads (*en julienne*). Blanch them in boiling salted water for 1 minute and drain. Stew the shallots in butter over a low flame. Pour over most of the stock and cider. Reduce the liquid by half. Cook the fillets of Dory in the liquid, remove them with a slotted spoon and keep hot. Reduce the liquid again to almost a glaze, stir in the double cream and reduce to a coating consistency. Add leeks and capsicum to the sauce. Check the seasoning and pour the sauce over or around the fish.

NOTE: if you want to serve pasta with this, choose fusilli, which will trap bits of shallot, leek and capsicum.

Grilled Red Mullet with Pickled 'Penny Buns'

Pickling time 4 days
450 g / 1 lb boletus mushrooms
½ lemon
450 ml / ¾ pint distilled vinegar
2 cloves garlic
1 bayleaf
1 pinch dried tarragon
½ teaspoon black peppercorns
sea salt
oil
8 small red mullet

Cut the gritty bases from the mushrooms (known familiarly as 'penny buns'). Wipe the mushrooms with a clean damp cloth. Slice the heads, cut out the spongy yellow part under the cap if they are large. Add the lemon juice to 600 ml / 1 pint of boiling water. Drop the mushrooms in the water and simmer 3 minutes. Drain. Add the vinegar, garlic, bayleaf and tarragon to the liquid. Roughly crush the peppercorns and add them to the liquid with a level teaspoon of salt. Reduce the liquid by a third. Fill a Kilner jar with the mushrooms, packing them tightly, and pour over the pickle. Pour a little oil on the pickle if you intend storing the mushrooms. Keep at least 4 days before using, weeks would be better.

Scale the mullet, but do not gut them. Brush with oil and grill or barbecue them for about 7 minutes, depending on their size. Sprinkle with sea salt. Serve with a generous spoonful of mushrooms and a little of their pickling liquor.

45

Mullet Braised with Sorrel

1 grey mullet weighing about
   1.35 kg / 3 lb
salt, pepper
115 g / 4 oz butter
1 teaspoon each shredded sorrel,
   chervil, chives
4 shallots, diced
1 Bramley apple
300 ml / ½ pint dry cider
450 g / 1 lb sorrel
1 teaspoon caster sugar
50 g / 2 oz clotted cream

Use enamel, tinned, stainless steel or non-stick pans with sorrel. Aluminium turns it black. Stainless steel knives are preferable to carbon steel for the same reason. Sorrel contains oxalic acid which can be poisonous taken in large doses. The wild variety is more sour, so presumably more suspect. Its leaves do not melt when cooked as do cultivated sorrel leaves.

Scale and remove the head and tail of the mullet. Season the inside. Combine 30 g / 1 oz of softened butter with the shredded sorrel, chervil and chives. Fill the belly cavity.

Sweat the shallots in half the remaining butter. When they soften add the flesh of the apple cut up small. Stew until soft and fluffy. Transfer to an ovenproof dish big enough to take the fish. (Cut the fish in half if in doubt.) Put the fish on the bed of apple. Pour over the cider and an equal quantity of water. Cover with buttered foil. Bake 25 minutes in a hot oven, 220°C, 425°F, gas mark 7.

Meanwhile finely chop the sorrel, and stew it in the remaining butter. Add the cooking liquid from the fish and boil to reduce by approximately two-thirds. Check the flavour and add the sugar. Beat in the clotted cream but do not let it boil. Serve the fish and sauce separately.

Roast Skate with Glazed Onions and Elderberry Vinegar

220 g / 8 oz sliced onion
80 g / 3 oz butter
1 heaped teaspoon soft brown
   sugar
2 tablespoons elderberry vinegar
200 ml / 7 fl oz fish stock
salt, pepper
1.35 kg / 3 lb skate wing

It's simplicity itself to make elderberry vinegar. Rinse two or three sprays of ripe elderberries. Dry them and place in a jar. Pour boiling red wine vinegar over them. Seal and leave in a sunny spot for at least a fortnight before broaching. The vinegar should keep for years.

Stew the onions very, very gently in a covered pan with 2 tablespoons of water for 40 minutes. Remove the lid and add a third of the butter and the sugar. Cook the onions until they brown and glaze. Stir in the elderberry vinegar with some of the berries and 4 tablespoons of fish stock. Boil hard for 1 minute and season.

Put the rest of the stock and the butter in a shallow roasting tin. Lay the trimmed skate wing on it with the white skin uppermost. Bake 15 minutes in a hot oven, 220°C, 425°F, gas mark 7. Scrape off the skin and baste the skate. Continue baking 10–15 minutes more. Glaze under a hot grill. Divide the skate into 4 portions and spoon over the onion and elderberry sauce.

Skate with Cheddar Cheese

1 teaspoon vinegar
4 × 175 g / 6 oz skate wings
600 ml / 1 pint milk
salt, pepper
40 g / 1½ oz butter
1 tablespoon chopped chives
115 g / 4 oz mature Cheddar, grated

Fishmongers normally skin one side of a skate, but leave the white skin on the belly. This is usually slimy, but by washing it you wash away most of the fish's flavour. Cover the bottom of a frying pan with water and a teaspoon of vinegar. Lay the skate wings in it skin side down. Cover with foil, simmer 5 minutes and drain. Scrape away the white skin. Now transfer the skate to a pan with the milk. Season and simmer until cooked, about 10 minutes.

Butter an ovenproof dish large enough to take the fish. Heat the oven to its highest temperature. Pour half a cupful of the milk in which the skate was cooked into the dish. Add the chives and half the cheese. Lay the fish on top and sprinkle with the rest of the cheese. Bake just long enough for the cheese to bubble without colouring and serve at once.

NOTE: the milk and cheese in the dish will separate (which I don't mind), but it can be stabilized by mixing a teaspoon of arrowroot with the milk before baking.

Soft Roes and Puff-ball

1 giant puff-ball
115 g / 4 oz butter
450 g / 1 lb soft herring roes
sea salt, pepper
50 g / 2 oz flour
2 tablespoons oil
2 tablespoons hazelnut oil

Cut 4 thickish slices from the puff-ball. Brush them with melted butter and put under a hot grill for about 3 minutes. Cut each one into 4 segments as you would a cake or tart.

Dip the herring roes in seasoned flour and fry them in oil and remaining butter until lightly browned. Drain them on absorbent paper and season generously.

Warm the hazelnut oil, not much above 30°C / 85°F, i.e. below body heat. Arrange the roes on four plates garnished with quarters of puff-ball and spoon over the oil. Grind a little sea salt over them and serve.

Seatrout Fillets Braised in Wooton Vineyard's Müller-Thurgau Wine

4 × 150 g / 5 oz seatrout fillets
50 g / 2 oz carrot
50 g / 2 oz celery
50 g / 2 oz leek
50 g / 2 oz large mushroom caps
salt, pepper
40 g / 1½ oz butter, melted
4 teaspoons diced shallots
1 lemon
4 sprigs thyme
4 tablespoons Müller-Thurgau
   wine (or Riesling)

Skin and lightly flatten the seatrout fillets. Cut the carrot, celery, leek and mushroom into matchsticks. Blanch them for a minute in salted water and drain.

For each portion, brush a square sheet of foil large enough to wrap a trout fillet with melted butter. Put a fillet in the centre of each sheet, with the vegetables around it. Season liberally. Sprinkle the diced shallots over the fillets. Cut the lemon into 8 slices and lay 2 overlapping slices on each fillet. Put a sprig of thyme on top. Wrap up the foil parcels, leaving the top of one corner open to act as a funnel. Pour a tablespoon of wine through the gap and seal the foil. Bake 8–10 minutes in a hot oven, 220°C, 425°F, gas mark 7.

NOTE: Müller-Thurgau is a wine grape commonly planted in England's southwest vineyards. It's a cross of Riesling and Sylvaner grapes, but rather easier to grow in our uncertain climate.

Stuffed Dabs with Speckled Mushroom Sauce

4 large dabs
150 g / 5 oz field mushrooms
80 g / 3 oz shallots
70 g / 2½ oz butter
1 clove garlic, crushed
¼ lemon
30 g / 1 oz breadcrumbs
20 g / ⅔ oz flour
200 ml / 7 fl oz chicken stock
80 ml / 3 fl oz milk
2 spring onions, chopped
115 g / 4 oz clotted cream
salt, pepper

Fillet the dabs and skin the black-skinned fillets. Dice the mushrooms and shallots till they are like breadcrumbs. Melt 40 g / 1½ oz butter in a pan and sweat the shallots and mushrooms 10 minutes. Take out a tablespoon of the mixture and set aside. Add garlic and the grated zest and juice of the lemon to the remainder. Cook over a low heat 10 minutes longer, stir in the breadcrumbs and season.

Make a roux with the remaining butter and the flour. Blend in the chicken stock and milk. Simmer 30 minutes, topping up with extra milk if necessary.

Add the spring onions to the sauce with the tablespoon of mushrooms and shallots which you have set aside. Whisk the cream into the sauce and season. Do not boil.

Put the white-skinned fillets on a sheet of buttered foil, skin down. Spread stuffing on them and put the remaining fillets on top like a sandwich. Cover with another sheet of buttered foil and bake 12 minutes in a very hot oven, 230°C, 450°F, gas mark 8. Arrange the stuffed dabs on a dish. Whisk any liquid on the foil into the sauce. Pour over the fish.

Turbot Darnes in Perry

1 pear (Conference or Bartlett)
sugar
¼ lemon
4 turbot darnes weighing about 175 g / 6 oz each
150 ml / ¼ pint + 1 tablespoon perry
2 diced shallots
300 ml / ½ pint double cream
salt, pepper
chopped chives

A darne of turbot is a cut made by splitting the backbone and dividing each half of the fish into sections. If you buy part of a turbot pursuade your fishmonger to give you the head. Even be prepared to pay him for it. Make a light stock by simmering the head with 450 ml / ¾ pint of water for 20 minutes.

Poach the pear in syrup allowing 300 g / 10 oz sugar per 600 ml / 1 pint of liquid. Add a squeeze of lemon juice. When the pear is tender drain and then slice.

Poach the turbot in 150 ml / ¼ pint of perry and 150 ml / ¼ pint of stock. The darnes will take about 10 minutes. Take the fish out of the stock with a slotted spoon and peel away the skin. Keep hot. Add the shallots to the stock and reduce it to a glaze. Add the cream and reduce it to a coating consistency. Stir in the tablespoon of perry and adjust the seasoning. Pour a cordon of sauce on four plates with the turbot in the middle. Garnish with sliced pear and sprinkle chives over the sauce.

NOTE: Perry, good perry that is, is becoming rare. The Fruit and Cider Institute at Long Ashton outside Bristol still makes and sells it as a flourishing cottage industry.

Baked Bass Fillets with Rosemary Jelly

Make the rosemary jelly in advance. Boil 450 g / 1 lb of chopped Bramley apples (skin, core, pips and all) with a teaspoon of lemon juice. Pour the pulp and juice rendered on to a sheet of muslin fastened over a bowl. Let the juice strain for an hour or so, then measure it. Pour it into a fresh pan and for every 50 ml / 2 fl oz juice add 40 g / 1½ oz sugar. Boil to setting point (i.e. 105°C, 220°F). Stir in a teaspoon of chopped rosemary and half a teaspoon of green peppercorns. Pour the hot jelly on to a shallow tray (so that the herbs are evenly distributed through the jelly when set). Leave to set.

49

Mix a tablespoon of chopped parsley with 30 g / 1 oz of wholemeal breadcrumbs. Add the grated zest of a small lemon, a crushed garlic clove and a pinch of sea salt. Reserve.

Brush four 150 g / 5 oz fillets of bass with melted butter and put them on a baking tray. Sprinkle the breadcrumb mixture over them. Bake 15 minutes in a hot oven, 220°C, 425°F, gas mark 7. Arrange on four dinner plates and serve with the jelly.

Brill Fillets with Wholegrain Mustard Sauce

1 × 2 kg / 4–5 lb brill
45 g / 1½ oz butter
2 diced shallots
2 tablespoons dry white wine
2 heaped teaspoons wholegrain mustard
175 ml / 6 fl oz double cream
5 sorrel leaves, chopped
1 tablespoon cognac
salt, pepper

Fillet and skin the brill. Put the head, bones and skin in a pan with 600 ml / 1 pint of water. Bring to the boil, skim and simmer 20 minutes. Strain the stock and pour three-quarters of it into a baking tray; cool. Lay the fillets on the tray and cover with buttered greaseproof paper. Reduce the remaining stock to a glaze with shallots and wine. Bake the fillets 12 minutes in a hot oven, 220°C, 425°F, gas mark 7. Pour the liquid from the tray into the pan with the glaze and reduce again. Stir in the mustard, cream and sorrel. Reduce to a light coating consistency, add the cognac and season. Beat in the remaining butter. Place the fillets on four plates. Pour the sauce over and serve.

For brussels sprout pudding
350 g / 12 oz brussels sprouts
40 g / 1½ oz butter
1 egg + 1 yolk

As an accompaniment, you may like to try this brussels sprout pudding. Cook the sprouts for 12 minutes in boiling salted water. Drain and blend to a purée with butter and eggs. Spoon into buttered ramekins and bake 40 minutes in a bain-marie in a moderate oven, 190°C, 375°F, gas mark 5. Turn out on to the dish containing the fish.

Mackerel

Presently she went to a cupboard which is also a coal-hole and brought out an immense frying pan, black both inside and out. She heated it till the fat ran, wiped it out with a newspaper, then placed in it three split mackerel.

Stephen Reynolds, *A Poor Man's House*

Cookery's cupboard is overstocked with myths; dover soles taste better four or five days out of the water; roast beef must go in a hot oven to seal in the juices; game should hang until high. On the fringe of such flawed saws is a belief that mackerel snared in a net tastes less good than one on the end of a hook. Three-star restaurants advertise *maquereau de ligne* as a speciality, justifying in the process an inflated price tag.

It is true that a mackerel, mangled in a trawl with a hundred tons of other fish, may be crushed and bruised. Netted by an inshore fisherman with small nets and a smaller catch it may be perfect. What matters more is freshness. Mackerel are oily, like pilchards, herring and sprat. Their flavour deteriorates more rapidly than white fish. On a warm summer day, a few hours lying on the deck of an open boat can prove fatal to them. The iridescent sheen on the skin dulls; flesh becomes fishy and unappetizing.

It is hard to imagine how mackerel fished off the southwest coast can taste sweet on a London fishmonger's slab. Nor, however refined the cuisine, will it taste as good in Lyons or Paris as it can along the Breton coast.

Just as milk fresh from the cow rewards the dairy farmer for his pains, but remains a mystery to 99 per cent of the population, so mackerel, straight out of the sea, belongs exclusively to those who catch it or those who have immediate access to the fisherman's haul.

You can buy mackerel for half the price of cod. At the turn of this century, fisherwomen hawked it for tuppence ha'penny a pair. From Brixham to Weymouth the poor ate mackerel as a staple, like those on the east coast ate herring.

Few would have bothered with rhubarb or gooseberry sauce. These fruits have been linked to mackerel for hundreds of years on the assumption that they will do for it what apple sauce does for goose or pork. Instead a splash of vinegar went into the frying pan and the juices were mopped up with bread at the end of the meal. Still on the oil and vinegar theme, there are alternative ways of pickling mackerel. One is to leave the fillets to steep for two or three days in a spiced and sweetened vinegar solution. The acid effectively cooks the raw fish. The other is to souse whole mackerel by poaching or stewing them in wine and vinegar, lemon juice or a dry cider.

Kauteriad (cotriade), Brittany's national fish stew, has a similar principle. Mackerel is cooked in a soup of stock and Muscadet. The pieces are drained and baptized in a vinaigrette containing plenty of shallots and parsley. And the soup is eaten as a second course. Despite its reputation for richness, mackerel contains roughly half the fat of an average hamburger. Nobody is going to drop down dead with a heart attack if, once in a while, he decides to fry his mackerel in bacon dripping. Nor will he suffer by baking it with olive oil and fresh thyme. To come clean, a mustard sauce, made from a reduction of cream and wine and enriched with fresh butter to give the sauce a gloss, contains a far more deadly concentration of saturated fats.

By itself, smoked mackerel is greasy. The fillets are, for the most part, sprayed with azo dyes, which gives them a garish appearance. Whole fish may be no better. There is little way of discerning whether the fish was fresh when smoked. If the belly walls are black or discoloured, it was starting to decay. Otherwise, the only clue is in the eating, by which time it's too late to do anything but complain.

Mackerel cruise the southwest throughout the year, but there used to be, and to some extent still is, a prejudice against eating it in winter. In the West Country it did not come into season until the 23rd chapter of Numbers was read in church, around 12th March. They are at their peak towards the end of summer. The high season coincides with the runs of sprats through the Channel, so setting sprats to catch mackerels has a factual basis.

Marinated Mackerel

4 × 300 g / 10 oz mackerel
salt
115 g / 4 oz onion
300 ml / ½ pint vinegar
2 tablespoons dry white wine
1 scant tablespoon caster sugar
1 scant teaspoon green
   peppercorns
1 dill stalk, chopped

Fillet the mackerel and rub them with salt. Slice the onion as thinly as you can and spread it over the fish. Leave for an hour. Combine the remaining ingredients and pour the pickle over the fillets, which should be completely immersed. Marinate at least 3 days before serving. Turn the fillets in the marinade once or twice during the marinating period.

Once marinated the mackerel will keep for several weeks. You can serve it cut into strips with salads, with toast or bread or by itself.

Split Mackerel and Pecan Sauce

Gut 4 mackerel and cut off the heads and tails. Open them up from the vent to the tail. Split them open as though you were going to kipper them. Remove the bones along one side of the fillet. Slide the knife under the other bones which are still attached to the backbone and cut them out with the backbone still attached. The pairs of fillets should remain in a single piece. This may sound complicated if you are unused to dealing with fish. Should you be in doubt, simply fillet the fish.

Chop 50 g / 2 oz of shelled pecan nuts in the blender. It does not matter if a few bits are not thoroughly mashed. Beat into the nuts a tablespoon of hazelnut oil, one crushed garlic clove, 1½ tablespoons of red wine vinegar and a little salt. Now beat into this stiff paste, a tablespoon at a time, some cold water until the mixture thins out to a dropping consistency.

Brush the mackerel with oil and either grill or fry them. Cook for one minute with the skin side closer to the heat, turn them and continue until done, about 10 minutes in all.

Carefully lift each pair of fillets on to hot plates. Spoon the sauce down through the middle of the fish.

NOTE: a good alternative to pecans are pistachio nuts added to a thickish hollandaise sauce.

Mackerel Baked with Lemon and Mustard

Whisk 6 tablespoons of Dijon mustard with the juice of 3 lemons and a little water. Put the mixture in a pan and bring it to the boil.

Butter an ovenproof dish. Gut mackerel. Cut off the heads and tails and split them along the back. Season. Bake 5 minutes in a hot oven, 220°C, 425°F, gas mark 7.

Pour the mustard and lemon mixture over the fish and return them to the oven to finish cooking, about 10 minutes more. Baste them once.

Transfer the mackerel to plates or serving dishes. Whisk the cooking juices left in the bottom of the dish, which will emulsify slightly. Check its seasoning. Pour it over the mackerel and serve.

Mackerel Tartlets with Baby Squid

40 g / 1½ oz butter
30 g / 1 oz chopped streaky
   bacon, rind removed
30 g / 1 oz finely diced onion
1 small pinch chopped rosemary
1 tablespoon dry white wine
2 tomatoes, skinned, seeded,
   chopped
salt, pepper
1 mackerel
6 baby squid
12 basil leaves

For the pastry:
350 g / 12 oz flour
200 g / 7 oz butter
2 eggs

Fishermen sometimes catch baby squid in their fine-meshed nets when they trawl for sprats. The squid sacs are no longer than a finger. To prepare them, or any squid, cut the tentacles off above the eyes. Scoop out the contents of the sacs and discard them together with the heads. Use only the sacs and tentacles, preferably unwashed.

Make a rich shortcrust pastry with flour, butter and eggs. Line four 10-cm / 4-inch tartlet tins with pastry (you will have some left over but it is not so easy to make small quantities of pastry). Let it rest half an hour. Line with greaseproof paper and beans and bake the pastry blind, about 20 minutes, in a moderately hot oven, 200°C, 400°F, gas mark 6, removing the paper and baking beans after 15 minutes.

Melt a knob of butter in a pan and add the bacon and onion. Cook till soft and then add the rosemary. Deglaze with white wine and add the tomato. Season lightly and stew over a low heat.

Brush the mackerel with the remaining butter and bake it in the oven 20 minutes (you could do this with the pastry). Remove the skin and flake the flesh. Add the flesh and squid to the pan with the tomatoes, just long enough for them to heat through. Stir in some basil, spoon the filling into the tartlets and serve.

Mackerel in Bacon Fat with Stewed Cranberries

220 g / 8 oz cranberries
50 g / 2 oz sugar
175 g / 6 oz green streaky bacon
    in one piece
a little oil or bacon fat
4 × 300 g / 10 oz mackerel
salt, black pepper
1 tablespoon flour

Serving gooseberries, which the French call 'currants for mackerel', with mackerel to cut their oiliness has become, if not a cliché, at least a long-established practice. It goes back at least to the 18th century. Cranberries, too, are good with this fish and the colour contrast on the plate is pleasing.

Put the cranberries in a small pan with a little water and the sugar. Bring to the boil and simmer until the cranberries start to split.

Remove the rind and then dice the bacon; fry it slowly in a large pan with a little oil or bacon fat until the bits are nice and crisp. Remove from the pan with a slotted spoon. Fillet the mackerel and dust them with seasoned flour. Fry them in the bacon fat. Drain and grind pepper over them, sprinkle the crisp bacon on top. Serve with stewed cranberries.

Mackerel and Grilled Aubergine with Apricot Compote

2 aubergines
salt, pepper
4 × 300 g / 10 oz mackerel
3 tablespoons olive oil
3 tablespoons chopped parsley

For the compote of apricots:
115 g / 4 oz dried apricots
    (soaked overnight)
1 lemon
1 tablespoon caster sugar
10 coriander seeds

Slice the aubergines in rings about 5 mm / ¼ inch thick. Salt them and let them stand in a colander for an hour. Rinse, press out most of the moisture and pat dry.

Gut and wipe the mackerel. Make a couple of lateral slashes with a sharp knife on both sides. Season them inside and out and brush with olive oil.

Brush the aubergines with oil. Grill or barbecue them about 6 minutes on each side. Grill the mackerel for about 8 minutes. Lay the aubergines on a plate and cover liberally with parsley and pepper. Lay the mackerel on top.

Serve with a compote of apricots which has to be made in advance. Put the apricots in a pan with the thinly sliced lemon, sugar, coriander and enough water to cover. Boil and simmer 30 minutes, by which time most of the liquid will have evaporated. Chill thoroughly before serving.

Mackerel with Orange and Cinnamon

300 ml / ½ pint Muscadet
2 tablespoons Chambéry
1 onion, quartered
1 leek, coarsely chopped
1 red capsicum, quartered
1 teaspoon tomato purée
½ stick of cinnamon
4 mackerel, gutted
salt, pepper
1 orange
15 g / ½ oz butter

Make a court bouillon with the wine, Chambéry, onion, leek, capsicum, tomato purée and cinnamon. Bring it to the boil then simmer 10 minutes.

Cut the heads and tails off four mackerel. Place in an ovenproof dish and pour the stock over them. Season. Slice the orange and arrange the slices on the mackerel. Cover with buttered foil. Bake 15 minutes in a hot oven, 220°C, 425°F, gas mark 7. Serve hot or chilled.

NOTE: a dry vermouth can be used instead of Chambéry.

Braised Mackerel on a Bed of Buttered Parsnips and Crab

4 × 300 g / 10 oz mackerel, gutted
200 ml / 7 fl oz dry white wine
200 ml / 7 fl oz white wine vinegar
salt, pepper
220 g / 8 oz parsnips
30 g / 1 oz butter
1 tablespoon double cream
115 g / 4 oz white crabmeat

Cut the heads off the mackerel and put the fish in an ovenproof dish, half covered with a mixture of wine and vinegar. Cover them with foil and braise 20 minutes in a moderate oven, 190°C, 375°F, gas mark 5, turning carefully after 10 minutes. Drain the mackerel and season lightly; keep hot.

Meanwhile, boil the parsnips in salted water. Drain and mash with butter. Fold in cream and crabmeat. Spoon some of the mixture on to four plates and lay the mackerel beside it.

Soused Mackerel with Lentils

4 × 300 g / 10 oz mackerel
175 g / 6 oz green lentils
salt, pepper
1 medium onion, chopped
1 teaspoon English mustard
1 tablespoon *vieux vinaigre de vin*
3½ tablespoons sunflower oil
4 gherkins, diced
300 ml / ½ pint vinegar
1 tablespoon sugar
2 bayleaves
1 tablespoon chopped parsley

Gut the mackerel and cut off heads and tails. Slit them along the backbone. Cook the lentils in boiling salted water. The time will vary according to their freshness and quality. Combine the onion with mustard, 1 tablespoon vinegar, oil, salt and pepper. Combine the dressing and gherkins with the lentils.

Boil the vinegar with an equal quantity of water, salt, sugar and bayleaves. Put the mackerel in a dish, pour over the pickle and bake uncovered in a hot oven, 220°C, 425°F, gas mark 7 for 15 minutes. Lay them on a bed of warm lentils and sprinkle with parsley.

Ginger Soused Mackerel

4 × 350 g / 12 oz mackerel
2 teaspoons cornflour
4 cloves garlic, finely chopped
1 × 5-cm / 2-inch piece of fresh
   ginger, finely diced
2 teaspoons soft brown sugar
2 teaspoons vinegar
2 tablespoons dry white wine
300 ml / ½ pint water
2 tablespoons chilli oil
salt, black pepper
6 spring onions, chopped

Gut the mackerel, cut off the heads and tails and split them along the backbone. Score the flesh on both sides and rub black pepper into the cuts.

Dissolve the cornflour in four teaspoons of water. Combine garlic, ginger, sugar, vinegar, wine and water.

Brush the fish with chilli oil. Fry about 1 minute on either side. Pour the liquid over them and add some salt. Simmer until cooked, turning from time to time. Take the fish out of the liquid and keep hot. Thicken the sauce with cornflour. Stir in the spring onions, check seasoning and leave just long enough to heat through. Pour the sauce over and around the fish and serve.

NOTE: this is an unashamed borrowing of Chinese cooking techniques. To make chilli oil, chop up dried chillies and put them into a neutral oil with their seeds. Leave for about a fortnight before using. The number of chillies depends on how hot you like your food. One chilli per 150 ml / ¼ pint of oil will suit most of us.

Spring Carrot and Mackerel Terrine

450 g / 1 lb young carrots
4 × 300 g / 10 oz mackerel
sea salt
6 egg yolks
15 g / ½ oz butter
4 scallops
½ lemon
1 tablespoon olive oil

For the sauce:
150 g / 5 oz mayonnaise
150 g / 5 oz strained Greek
   yoghourt
15 g / ½ oz watercress leaves
2 tablespoons chopped tarragon
2 tablespoons chopped chives

Rinse the carrots, put them in a bowl and cover with boiling water. Leave a minute, drain and rub off the skins. Split them lengthwise. Fillet the mackerel, skin them; the results won't be visible, so don't worry if a little skin still adheres to the fillets. Put them in a food processor with half a teaspoon of salt. Blend them to a paste, then beat in the egg yolks. Line a rectangular terrine with buttered foil or non-stick baking parchment. Lay a row of carrots along the bottom. Cover with half the puréed mackerel. Slice the scallops and layer them over the mackerel. Squeeze lemon juice on them and drizzle olive oil over them. Arrange the rest of the carrots on top and then the remaining purée. Cover the terrine with buttered foil, parchment or greaseproof paper and a lid. Stand the terrine in a tray of simmering water. Cook 30 minutes in a hot oven, 220°C, 425°F, gas mark 7. Test whether the terrine is cooked with a skewer (as you would a cake). Place a weight on the terrine and chill overnight before turning out.

Combine the mayonnaise and yoghourt. Blanch the

watercress and herbs for 10 seconds. Rinse under cold water, dry and rub through a sieve. Fold into the mayonnaise and yoghourt.

Mackerel Stew with Peas

1 large onion, chopped
2 tablespoons sunflower or groundnut oil
450 g / 1 lb small new potatoes
4 cloves garlic, finely chopped
salt, black pepper
1 fennel stalk
1 sachet saffron
450 g / 1 lb shelled peas
4 × 300 g / 10 oz mackerel
4 eggs

Fry the onion in oil until it starts to soften, then add the potatoes. Cook for a couple of minutes and add the garlic. Cover the potatoes and onions with water, bring to the boil, add salt, the fennel and the saffron. Simmer 5 minutes and add the peas.

Meanwhile, gut the mackerel and cut off heads and tails. Add the fish to the stew and cook 10 minutes more.

Poach the eggs in a separate pan of simmering water; drain them with a slotted spoon.

Put the stew of mackerel, potatoes and peas in broad-rimmed old-fashioned soup dishes with some of their cooking liquid. Add the eggs and finish with a little black pepper.

Grilled Mackerel with Caponata

3 anchovy fillets
salt and pepper
220 g / 8 oz aubergine
1 small stick celery, chopped
1 large onion, sliced
6 black olives
6 green olives
1 beef tomato
6 tablespoons olive oil
1 teaspoon soft brown sugar
1 tablespoon red wine vinegar
2 teaspoons capers (preserved in salt)
4 mackerel

Caponata is a kind of Sicilian ratatouille. Pound the anchovies to a paste. Wash, peel, cube and salt the aubergine. Leave it an hour in a colander, and squeeze out some of the moisture it contains. Pit the olives. Squeeze the seeds and juice from the tomato and liquidize the flesh.

Heat 2 tablespoons of olive oil in a pan and stew the celery 10 minutes over a very low heat, then add onion and continue cooking until the onion becomes transparent. Fry the aubergine in oil in a second pan over a high heat until it colours but does not burn. Sprinkle sugar over it, when it is melted add the vinegar, tomatoes, olives, anchovies, a sprinkling of pepper and the capers (preserved in brine, not vinegar). As soon as this mixture is hot, scrape it into the pan with the onion and celery. Stew very slowly for 2 hours and season. Watch out for sticking.

Brush the mackerel with the remaining oil, score the flesh both sides and grill them, ideally over charcoal, for 10 minutes. Serve them with the caponata, which may be either hot or cold.

Designer Salads

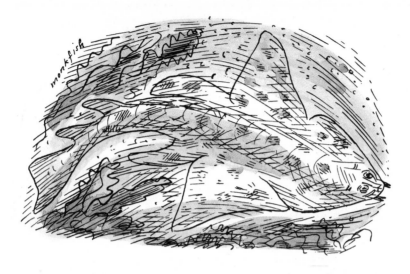

'How do you manage to introduce such a delicious flavour into your salads?'
'Ah! that should be my secret,' was the reply. 'But I will tell him to you.
After I have made all my preparations, and the green food is mixed with the
dressing, I chew a little clove of garlic between my teeth—so—and then
breathe gently over the whole.'

Recipe attributed to Charles Elme Francatelli, the Reform Club chef,
by Edward Spencer in *Cakes and Ale*

In one sector of the octagonal plate lies a curlicue of radicchio and beside it an artichoke heart sliced and spread apart like a lady's fan. Next to it a spray of chicory climbs upwards like the wave of a Hokusai print. In its wash stands a neat, sculpted cherry tomato and beside it a single violet asparagus tip. Next to that is variegated oakleaf lettuce, whose auburn autumnal tints contrast with a pair of ebony *trompettes de la mort*. Alone in the centre of this edible picture frame, a single perfect slice of lobster. 'Eat me! Eat me!' it seems to cry. Bunkum!

Modern salads have been hand-crafted to suit food poseurs. Itsy-bitsy, teeny-weeny pretentious morsels are exhibited as culinary art. There is worse to come. It will be made clear to the eater that to obtain the ultimate orgiastic pleasure he must dissect a piece of each ingredient, prepare a cocktail on the end of his fork which, once purveyed to his mouth, he must chew with reverence.

Yet, for all its pseudo-Japanese sparseness, salade nouvelle can teach something—freshness for a start, and colour, and texture and variety.

Salad, the word, has centuries since broken adrift from its original attachment to the latin *sal*—salt, but it is worth speculating on why the link existed in the first place. Most of us have wandered into the kitchen on a sweltering summer day, cut an inch of cucumber, dipped it in salt and popped it in our mouth. Without salt the cucumber would be insipid; with it, it tastes refreshing. Tossing a salad in a dressing turns lifeless 'herbaceous meat' fit for nobody but Peter Rabbit into something toothsome.

Two French words, *touiller* and *fatiguer*, are both à propos in describing the salad maker's art, or lack of it. It is vital to *touiller*, but not so much that you *fatiguer*. In other words, the salad needs plenty of turning, but not so much that it becomes tired.

The proverb that you must ask a miser to pour the vinegar, a spendthrift the oil and a sage the salt, if you want a good dressing, holds good. It is a curious social phenomenon that some medieval salads were dressed only with vinegar (cousins of mint sauce?) whereas some modern ones contain only oil as a dressing. Two parts vinegar to one of oil was common until World War II. Now, four, five and six measures of oil are often recommended.

But which oil?

It depends on how you mean to use it. If it is merely a lubricant which helps to bring other flavours together, a tasteless groundnut or sunflower oil is fine. Corn oil is anathema because it leaves a lipsalve-like film on the lips and in the mouth. If the oil has a positive influence on a mixed salad's taste then it is time to graduate to olive and nut oils.

Composing a mixed salad, one that contains fish, has its own set of ground-rules. First, you must establish whether it is a little something for whetting the appetite, or one course among several, or a main dish. Is it something to serve in a bowl or on a plate?

Usually the fish is going to be the cornerstone, so you want enough of it in the recipe for it to be prominent, but not so much that you create a fish-plus-garnish equation where the latter is an insignificant adjunct. Think in terms of contrasts which combine to make wholes: white hake marinated in lemon juice on a ground of dark green Cos lettuce or tétragone rather than pale endive; the sweetness of scallops balanced with hazelnut oil and maybe bitter dandelion or lamb's lettuce. The size of different ingredients must also complement each other. It seems gross to spread a cabbage lettuce blanket over a plate. Rarely should you require more than a fork, or a pair of chopsticks, to tackle a salad. If the patchwork of tastes, hues, textures and tones makes a subtle whole, the presentation is in-built. It cannot be arranged to any better effect by an artistic designer. Salads are composed for the palate not the plate.

Baby Monkfish Salad with Dill

½ cucumber
salt, pepper
caul fat (see note)
1 tablespoon chopped dill leaves
450 g / 1 lb baby monkfish
1 beef tomato
1 young carrot
1 cos lettuce
1 tablespoon wine vinegar
1 tablespoon almond oil
3 tablespoons groundnut oil
50 g / 2 oz sweetcorn kernels, cooked
1 tablespoon chopped fresh herbs (dill, tarragon, parsley)
1 mint leaf, chopped

Peel and seed the cucumber. Cut the flesh into small cubes and salt it for 30 minutes.

Soak a large square of caul fat until it whitens. Drain, salt and sprinkle with dill. Lay a baby monkfish on it. Wrap it up in the caul and bake 20 minutes in a moderately hot oven, 200°C, 400°F, gas mark 6. Allow to cool.

Drop the tomato into boiling water for 12 seconds, drain, skin, seed, then dice the flesh. Grate the carrot and wash the lettuce. Rinse and pat dry the cucumber.

Make a dressing with the vinegar, oils, salt and pepper. Remove the fish from the caul and cut it into hazelnut-sized pieces. Toss the fish, vegetables and sweetcorn in dressing. Arrange on a bed of lettuce and garnish with chopped herbs.

NOTE: caul fat is available from small family butchers. It is commonly used to wrap faggots but it also makes a protective outer coat for tender fleshed fish.

Crab, Scallop and Pink Grapefruit Cocktail

6 lettuce leaves
1 pink grapefruit
4 scallops
115 g / 4 oz white crabmeat
150 ml / ¼ pint mayonnaise
salt, pepper

Joël Robuchon, probably the best chef in Paris at the moment, makes mayonnaise with grapeseed oil, because it does not separate when left to chill in the fridge. This is a great wheeze, because you can make pints of mayonnaise in advance and raid your store as and when you want it.

Shred the lettuce leaves and put them in the bottom of four large wine glasses. Cut the peeled pink grapefruit into segments on a plate; it will render plenty of juice.

Steam shelled scallops for 3–5 minutes. Dice the white meat. Marinate the white meat and the coral in grapefruit juice for 1 hour, then drain them on absorbent paper. Combine the diced scallops with crabmeat and mayonnaise. Season. Chop up all but four grapefruit segments. Mix with the shellfish and spoon on to the lettuce. Decorate each portion with a segment of grapefruit and the coral.

Crawfish Tail with Orange and Mint

Drop 4 small tomatoes into boiling water for 12 seconds. Drain and skin. Quarter them and remove the seeds. Sprinkle with a little sea salt.

Slice off both ends of 2 oranges. Stand them on a plate. Cut off the rind, at the same time removing the pith and skin around the individual segments. Cut out each segment using a sharp knife.

Remove the black thread running down the centre of a cooked crawfish tail and slice it. The tail should weigh about 220 g / 8 ounces.

Make a dressing: crush 3 small garlic cloves with a little sea salt. Chop up 3 teaspoons of fresh mint. Dice a small dried chilli. Combine these ingredients with the juice of a lime. Leave to macerate 1 hour. Beat together and spoon over the crawfish and the orange. Arrange the crawfish pieces neatly on a plate; lay the orange segments on them and garnish with tomato.

Crawfish Tail Salad with Basil Sauce

1 beef tomato
1 teaspoon sugar
1 tablespoon water
50 g / 2 oz mayonnaise
40 g / 1½ oz strained Greek
   yoghourt
40 ml / 1½ fl oz olive oil
1 teaspoon lemon juice
12 basil leaves, chopped
salt, pepper
salad leaves: chicory, Cos,
   radicchio, corn salad
220 g / 8 oz poached crawfish tail

Chop the tomato and put in a small pan with sugar and water; stew gently until most of the liquid has evaporated. Rub the small quantity of the remaining pulp through a sieve. Combine the mayonnaise and yoghourt. Beat in half the olive oil, the lemon juice and tomato pulp. Fold in the basil and season the sauce.

Wash and dry the salad leaves. Toss them in the remaining olive oil. Arrange them in four salad bowls. Shell the poached crawfish tail. Discard the thread of intestine. Dice the tail and combine it with the basil sauce. Spoon on to the bed of lettuce.

Hen Lobster Salad with Marigold Petals

Serves 2

1 × 700 g / 1 ½ lb hen lobster
  with eggs
salad leaves: Webbs Wonder,
  corn salad, Tom Thumb,
  oakleaf and Cos
4 nasturtium leaves
2 tablespoons chopped chives and
  fennel, mixed
salad burnet (optional)
½ teaspoon mustard
4 green peppercorns, crushed
1 tablespoon cider vinegar
4 tablespoons almond oil
sea salt
1 tablespoon marigold petals
black pepper

Put the lobster in a pan of cold salted water. Cover and bring to the boil. Simmer 13 minutes then drain. Break off the tail. Scrape the eggs from between the swimmerets. Shell the tail meat and slice it into thin collops. Crack the claws and remove the meat.

Wash the salad leaves, enough for two generous portions. Shred the nasturtium leaves. Mix half of the nasturtiums with the herbs.

Make a dressing with mustard, peppercorns, cider vinegar, almond oil and sea salt. Toss the salads and herbs in three-quarters of the dressing and arrange in two good sized salad bowls.

Brush the lobster collops with the rest of the dressing. Lay them on the salad. Sprinkle over the eggs, marigold petals and the last of the nasturtiums. Add pepper.

Herrings Pickled with Black, White and Green Peppercorns

Marinating time 4 days

1 teaspoon green peppercorns
½ teaspoon black peppercorns
½ teaspoon white peppercorns
400 ml / 14 fl oz seaweed vinegar
  (page 8)
5 tablespoons water
2 tablespoons soft brown sugar
2 bayleaves
½ teaspoon ground allspice
1 teaspoon mustard seeds
sea salt
4 herrings

Crush all the peppercorns together in a mortar. Prepare a marinade with the vinegar, water, sugar, bayleaves, allspice, mustard seeds, peppercorns and sea salt.

Fillet the herrings. Sprinkle sea salt over them and leave for 30 minutes. Pat them dry, put them in the marinade and leave at least 4 days before eating.

NOTE: a nice way of eating the herrings is with thick chunks of wholemeal bread and pieces of cucumber dipped in sea salt. Or they can be served with sea purslane salad: young sea purslane leaves picked from their stalks (hard to give a quantity for four, but about half a colander full with the stalks), 8 sprigs of rocket, ½ cucumber, 3 spring onions, 1 tablespoon pine kernel oil, 3 tablespoons sunflower oil, 1 tablespoon old wine vinegar, salt. Blanch the purslane leaves 1 minute in boiling salted water, drain, refresh under running water and pat dry. Peel, seed, and cut the cucumber into 5 mm / ¼ inch cubes, salt it for ½ hour; rinse and pat dry. Make a vinaigrette with the oils, vinegar and salt. Toss the purslane leaves, rocket, cucumber and chopped spring onions in the dressing. (I've also done this with garlic croûtons.)

Mackerel and Endive Salad

115 g / 4 oz smoked streaky
  bacon in one piece
1 teaspoon oil
1 mackerel
50 g / 2 oz Cheddar
curly endive leaves
4 tablespoons walnut oil
2 tablespoons sunflower oil
2 tablespoons wine vinegar
salt, pepper

Derind the bacon and cut it across the grain into lardons roughly half the size of a lady's little finger. Heat the teaspoon of oil in a frying pan and sauté the lardons until well coloured. Remove from the pan and reserve them on absorbent paper. Top and tail the mackerel. Score the flesh on both sides. Fry the mackerel in the pan used for the lardons. It will take little more than 10 minutes. Split open the mackerel, pull out the backbone and fins. Cut the fish into small gobbets. Cube the cheese.

Clean enough endive for four portions (green leaves are bitter, so choose the yellowish ones).

Make a vinaigrette with the oils, vinegar and seasoning. Go easy on the salt and add lots of freshly ground black pepper. Toss the lardons, endive and cheese in three-quarters of the dressing. Arrange on four plates with the mackerel on top and spoon over the remaining vinaigrette.

Prawn and Smoked Fish Salad with Yoghourt and Tomato Sauce

12 large prawns
salt, pepper
350 g / 12 oz smoked haddock
300 ml / ½ pint milk
1 smoked mackerel
2 tomatoes
300 ml / ½ pint goat's (or ewe's)
  yoghourt
¼ large red onion
½ teaspoon chopped tarragon
12 chopped basil leaves
assorted salad leaves

Boil the prawns for a couple of minutes and shell them. (You should add two level teaspoons of sea salt per 600 ml / 1 pint of water.) Poach the haddock in milk. Drain and flake it. Remove the skin and bones from the mackerel (smoked mackerel fillets are rarely as good as the whole fish). Flake the flesh.

Drop the tomatoes in boiling water for 12 seconds. Drain, skin, seed, then chop the flesh. Salt them and fold into the yoghourt. Dice the onion and fold it into the yoghourt together with the tarragon and basil torn into small bits. Season.

Decorate four plates or bowls with assorted salad leaves. Lay out the fish and shellfish on top. Spoon over the dressing.

Lemon Sole Salad

sunflower or groundnut oil
4 lemon sole fillets
115 g / 4 oz spinach
salt, pepper
sorrel (optional)
115 g / 4 oz mangetout peas
½ lemon
150 ml / ¼ pint double cream
1 tablespoon chopped fresh herbs
1 teaspoon chopped mint
2 teaspoons groundnut oil
1 teaspoon vinegar

Brush a large sheet of foil with oil. Flatten the sole fillets with a heavy bladed knife or cleaver. Pop the spinach into boiling salted water for 30 seconds; drain well. Lay the softened leaves over the sole fillets. If you have some sorrel, add one leaf per fillet. Roll up the fillets from head to tail. Season and lay them close together on the foil. Wrap up and bake 10 minutes in a hot oven, 200°C, 400°F, gas mark 6. Leave to cool in the foil.

Boil the mangetout in salted water 2–3 minutes; drain.

Whisk together the lemon juice, cream, herbs, salt and pepper. Blend the mint with the oil and vinegar. Unwrap the foil parcel. Slice each rolled fillet into 5 segments, as you would a swiss roll. Arrange them in rings on four plates. Cover with the cream dressing. Just before serving pile mangetout in the centre of each 'crown' and brush with minted vinegar.

Steamed Monkfish with a Red Cabbage Salad

220 g / 8 oz monkfish
¼ lemon
salt, pepper
350 g / 12 oz red cabbage
50 g / 2 oz finely diced onion
1–2 tablespoons lemon juice
1 teaspoon tarragon mustard
6 tablespoons groundnut oil
40 g / 1½ oz finely grated carrot
chervil

Apart from its outer skin, monkfish is covered in a highly elastic inner wetsuit, which is better pared away before cooking. The trick of cooking monkfish is that it should be just cooked through, when its flavour is pleasant and somewhat reminiscent of shellfish. Overcooked, you might as well buy rock salmon.

Having removed the elastic coat, steam the monkfish. The time will vary according to its thickness. Allow roughly 10 minutes per 2.5 cm / 1 inch at the thickest part. Cool slightly and carve into thin slices at right angles to the main bone (as you might carve a saddle of lamb). Squeeze lemon juice over the slices and season.

Shred the red cabbage with a stainless steel knife to prevent discolouration. Mix the onion with it. Make a dressing with lemon juice to taste, mustard and oil. Season the cabbage and toss it in the dressing. Just before serving fold in the grated carrot.

Pile the cabbage on four plates with the fish on top or round the sides and decorate with chervil.

Seatrout Marinated in St Raphaël

Marinating time 24 hours
650 g / 1½ lb seatrout
150 ml / ¼ pint white St Raphaël
150 ml / ¼ pint lemon juice
1 clove garlic, finely chopped
115 g / 4 oz finely diced white of leek
sea salt, cayenne pepper
Tabasco
350 g / 12 oz shelled peas
2 beef tomatoes
4 tablespoons double cream

St Raphaël, a French apéritif, contains quinine. You can buy a sweeter red or a bitter white. The white suits this recipe. The following anecdote appears in Pamela Vandyke Price's *Dictionary of Wines and Spirits*: 'There is a tradition that anyone who takes a lot will never go blind because, at the beginning of the 19th century, a Frenchman prayed successfully to St Raphaël to restore his sight (but evidence is not conclusive on the subject).'

Fillet the seatrout and cut it into chunks, 5 × 2.5 cm / 2 × 1 inch. Combine the St Raphaël and lemon juice, garlic, leek and sea salt plus a few dashes of Tabasco. Marinate the fish for 24 hours, turning it two or three times.

Boil the peas in salted water until tender, then drain. Drop the tomatoes in boiling water for 12 seconds. Peel, seed and sieve the flesh. Beat with cream and season with salt and cayenne.

Lay two or three pieces of fish per portion on a plate with a tablespoon of strained marinade. Garnish with peas and pour over the sauce.

Smoked Haddock and Fennel Salad

Bulbs of fennel vary in size, but try and find small ones which should be more tender.

Peel away the outer stems of 4 small fennel bulbs. Cut off the stalk, but reserve the leaves. Put a slice of lemon peel in a pan of boiling salted water. Add the fennel and boil 10 minutes. Drain. Cool. Slice them from root to stalk into thin slices which should keep their shape.

Take a large fillet of undyed smoked haddock, as freshly smoked as you can find it. Carve slices off this fillet as though you were carving a side of smoked salmon. Arrange the slices of haddock and fennel on four plates. Whisk 2 tablespoons of lemon juice into 4 tablespoons of olive oil. Spoon the dressing over the fish and fennel. Grind black pepper over the fish and garnish with sprigs of fennel leaves.

66

Steamed Scallop Salad with Hazelnuts and Tomato

12 scallops
1 beef tomato
24 hazelnuts, approx.
1 Webbs Wonder lettuce
1 heaped teaspoon diced shallot
1 tablespoon wine vinegar
salt
3 tablespoons hazelnut oil
1 tablespoon groundnut or
  sunflower oil

Open and clean the scallops in the usual way (page 15). Drop the tomato in boiling water for 12 seconds. Drain, peel, seed and cut the flesh into small pieces. Leave the hazelnuts for 7 minutes in a hot oven. Rub off the skins. Tear the washed lettuce leaves into mouth-sized pieces and arrange them on four plates (if the lettuce is on the large side you will not need all of it).

Beat the shallots, vinegar, salt and a tablespoon of tomato together. Then beat in the oils.

Slice the white flesh of the scallops in two. Steam them 3 minutes. Heap a small pile of tomato in the middle of the plates. Surround with a ring of scallops. Garnish with hazelnuts. Pour over the dressing and serve while the scallops are still warm.

The Answer Lies in the Oil

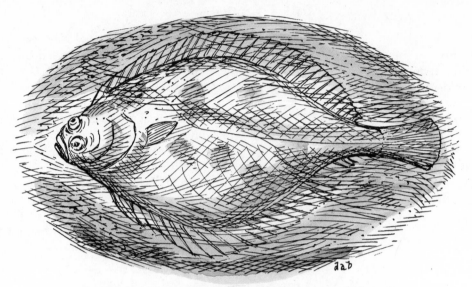

Fats are composed of the same three chemical elements as are the carbohydrates, namely, carbon, hydrogen and oxygen but in different proportions so that fats constitute a much more concentrated form of fuel than do carbohydrates.

Essentials of Nutrition by Henry Sherman and Caroline Sherman Langford

Chemically speaking, there is no essential difference between a fat such as butter and an oil. The polemics concerning their respective merits only flare up when the nutritionists argue about how much fat we should consume and whether saturated animal fats are more damaging in large doses than some of the polyunsaturated vegetable oils.

In the cooking arena much of this debate is a bright scarlet herring, but not all of it. Nobody will perish of arteriosclerosis as a result of gorging himself occasionally on butter sauce. Going down to the fish and chip shop three times a week may in the medium term prove fatal to thousands of people. If the chippy happens to be frying in beef dripping, their risk is certainly increased.

Fried food itself is not bad, any more than a lettuce leaf is good. How often you indulge and how you cook with oils and fat matter. For example, well over half the calories in battered fried fish derive from the oil. This alone should encourage anyone bothered even a teeny bit about their diet to eat vegetables, other than chips, and salad as a part of it. Similarly, tartare sauce made with an emulsion of oil is an odd accompaniment.

Why eat fried fish in the first place? The answer is simple—pleasure. Any food puritan who would gladly proscribe it all is carrying nutritional imperatives beyond the limits of a sensible balanced diet into the realms of irrational obsession. Such enthusiastic zeal would be better placed teaching cooks how to make better use of their oil rather than banning it. If a cook overloads a pan of oil with slabs of battered cod, the temperature of the oil drops dramatically, the fish boils in the oil and the batter soaks up the fat like blotting paper. The pieces may eventually turn crisp and golden, because the oil temperature is bound to rise, but when you cut into the batter on the plate, grease will ooze out like pus from a lanced boil.

Frying a fish in batter or breadcrumbs is like wrapping it in a Mae West—in reverse. The objective is to keep the moisture on the inside. To do that, the first contact between the oil and the coating is crucial; the outer skin must set so as to prevent the natural juices in the fish from escaping. This is only possible when the oil is hot enough. Preheating to 175°C, 350°F is a good rule of thumb temperature for most recipes. With that much heat most of the flavour in an oil will have been dissipated and you will not be able to tell whether you have been using a cheap corn oil or olive oil.

It is a good plan to allow five times the volume of oil to product. If your fish weighs 200 g / 7 oz, you must allow 1 litre / 1¾ pints of oil. That may sound wasteful, but if you fry wisely, you need never chuck out rancid, burnt or fishy oil. (Here is an old trick that works: if you are suspicious that the oil is tainted by a fishy odour, heat it gently, adding some croûtons of stale bread. The bread acts as a scapegoat and absorbs all the nasties.) The real technique of oil maintenance is to filter it after each use, to keep the frying basket clean, to scrub away the brown gums, and to top up with fresh oil before each fry-up.

If the flavour, in a positive sense, is important, you should heat it neither overlong nor overmuch. That is true of olive oil and most nut oils. Virgin olive oil has been pressed, like wine, once and without any form of heat treatment. It retains the aroma of the fruit. As with wine, the quality of this precious commodity varies. In Italy a single manufacturer may produce three or four versions of his virgin oil, more or less fruity and containing more or less of the pulpy deposit in the bottom of the bottle, depending on his customers' various preferences. The colour too may range from olive green to amber.

Nut oils vary as much in strength and quality. Low grade hazelnuts or walnuts are used, sometimes with the shells and nuts crushed together. Sometimes the end product is the combination of several pressings. The finest hazelnut and walnut oils are made from the best shelled nuts. They are roasted slowly and crushed in a stone mill which extracts the oil.

These speciality oils have a highly concentrated flavour. Very little goes a long way. The obvious time to reach for hazelnut oil is when making an autumnal salad, but nut oils can replace other fats to advantage. In trout with almonds, for instance, you can brush a little warmed almond oil over the cooked fish instead of dousing it in clarified butter. It's a solution which should offend nobody, least of all the entrenched food bigot.

Fried Dabs and Five Spice Sauce

4 dabs
½ lime
1 teaspoon dried yeast
250 ml / 9 fl oz water
200 g / 7 oz wholemeal flour
1 diced shallot
30 g / 1 oz butter
1 pinch five spice powder
½ tablespoon tomato purée
150 ml / ¼ pint dry white wine
150 ml / ¼ pint chicken stock
1 tablespoon anchovy essence
1 teaspoon cornflour
salt, pepper
oil for frying
1 egg white

Scrape the scales off the dabs, rinse them under running water and pat dry. Lift the fillets and squeeze lime juice over the flesh. Dissolve the yeast in water at body temperature. Beat in the flour. Leave in a warm place until the batter has trebled its volume.

Stew the shallot in butter and add the five spice powder. Stir in the tomato purée and let it cook for a minute, then add the wine and chicken stock. Beat in the anchovy essence, simmer 20 minutes and add cornflour dissolved in a little water. Check the seasoning.

Heat the frying oil. Whisk the egg white till stiff and fold it into the batter. Dip fillets in batter and fry until very crisp. Drain them on absorbent paper and salt lightly. Serve two fillets per portion and the sauce separately.

NOTE: five spice powder is a mixture of 5 different spices: anise pepper, star anise, cassia, cloves and fennel seed. It is unrelated to allspice.

Peal in Olive Oil

Peal is the local name along the southwest coast for sea-trout, and School Peal for the smaller seatrout that swim back up the rivers for the first time.

Make a classic court bouillon: put 1½ litres / 2½ pints of water in a large pan. Add an onion stuck with 2 cloves, a clove of garlic, a bouquet garni of thyme, bayleaf and parsley stalks, 2 teaspoons of peppercorns and 1 dried chilli. Bring to the boil, simmer 30 minutes and top up with a little extra water to replace any which has evaporated.

Drop 1 large piece of seatrout, weighing 1 kg / 2¼ lb into the court bouillon. It should be completely immersed. Simmer 15 minutes, then allow the fish to cool in the liquid. Drain the fish and remove the skin. Take out the bones being careful not to damage the fillets.

Scrub the skin of a lemon to remove all traces of diphenyl. Slice the lemon thinly.

Cover the bottom of a terrine with the fillets cut into 5 cm / 2 inch lengths. Cover with lemon slices. Pour over plenty of virgin olive oil (one of the best brands available in Britain and imported from France is L'Olivier). Continue alternating layers of fish and lemon with extra oil. Cover the terrine with a lid or a sheet of foil. Refrigerate 24 hours or more to allow the flavours to blend.

Goujonettes of Lemon Sole 'En Surprise'

2 lemon soles
100 g / 3½ oz goat's cheese
50 g / 2 oz smoked cod's roe
150 ml / ¼ pint milk
salt
175 g / 6 oz flour
4 eggs, beaten
wholemeal breadcrumbs
oil for frying

Fillet the lemon soles and cut them into bite-sized pieces. Slice the mould off a goat's cheese (one that is firm but not too hard and dry). Skin the roe and cut it into marble-sized bits.

Line up four small trays in front of you. Pour milk in the first, sifted, seasoned flour in the second, beaten egg in the third and breadcrumbs in the fourth.

Cube the cheese, pass it through milk, flour, egg, crumbs, and then once more in egg and crumbs. Coat the sole and roe in single layers of milk, flour, egg and crumbs. Deep-fry the fish, roe and cheese. The cheese takes about 4 minutes, the fish and roe a little less. Drain on absorbent paper and sprinkle with salt.

Serve with a green salad and a fresh tomato sauce.

Marinated Hake with Beetroot and Walnuts

Marinating time 2 hours
450 g / 1 lb hake fillets
½ lemon
1 lime
450 g / 1 lb cooked beetroot
1 large diced shallot
1 teaspoon Dijon mustard
1 tablespoon red wine vinegar
salt
3 tablespoons walnut oil
50 g / 2 oz coarsely chopped
   walnuts
chopped chives

Soak the skinned hake fillets in water 8 minutes. Drain and pat dry. Cut in 2.5 cm / 1 inch cubes. Squeeze lemon and lime juice over them and marinate 2 hours, turning every 30 minutes. Grate the cooked beetroot.

Combine the shallot with mustard and vinegar. Season and beat in the walnut oil. Toss the beetroot in the dressing. Taste the combination and add a little extra vinegar if you like.

Arrange the beetroot on a serving dish and sprinkle with walnuts. Arrange the fish slightly apart and sprinkle with chives. Don't give the beetroot the chance of staining the fish, which should be perfectly white.

Pout Whiting Fried with Almonds

4 pout whiting
salt, pepper
flour
50 ml / 2 fl oz sunflower oil
30 g / 1 oz flaked almonds
1 tablespoon lemon juice
1 egg yolk
130 ml / 4½ fl oz almond oil
115 ml / 4 fl oz groundnut or
   sunflower oil

Chubby pout whiting are only good to eat when they go straight from the net to the frying pan. After more than a day they become flavourless and cotton-woolly.

Score the whiting twice on each side of their flesh. Season them inside and out. Dust with flour. Fry them in sunflower oil, about 5 minutes on either side, then drain on absorbent paper. Toast the almonds under the grill.

Beat lemon juice and egg yolk together, then mix in the almond and groundnut oils. Season.

To serve, put the fish on preheated plates and brush the skin with slightly warmed oil. Sprinkle almonds over the top and offer the sauce separately.

Smoked Cod's Roe Fritters with Half-cooked Tomatoes

115 g / 4 oz butter
300 ml / ½ pint water
115 g / 4 oz plain flour
115 g / 4 oz smoked cod's roe,
   skinned
1 egg
oil for frying (preferably olive oil)
salt, cayenne pepper, pepper
2 tablespoons olive oil
1 clove garlic, crushed
3–4 coarsely chopped tomatoes

Add the cubed butter to a pan containing the water. Bring it quickly to a rolling boil and stir in the sifted flour. Beat the mixture off the heat until it leaves the pan sides. Transfer the piping hot mixture to a food processor and blend in the cod's roe. Add the egg and blend again. Chill the mixture.

Heat a pan of frying oil. Using a pair of teaspoons, form nuggets of paste and slide them into the hot oil. Fry 5 minutes until puffed up and golden. Drain on absorbent paper and sprinkle with salt and cayenne.

Heat 1 tablespoon of olive oil in a pan. Add the garlic and tomatoes. Fry for a couple of minutes until they start to soften. Season and drizzle the rest of the olive oil over them. Spread a layer of tomato on four plates and pile cod's roe fritters on top.

Soft Roe Fritters with Pistou

1 clove garlic
20 basil leaves, approx.
1 tablespoon olive oil

Pound the garlic, basil, olive oil and parmesan to a paste with a little sea salt. If you want to soften the pistou add fresh goat's cheese.

72

1 tablespoon freshly grated
    parmesan
sea salt
1 tablespoon fresh goat's cheese
    (optional)
450 g / 1 lb soft roes
115 g / 4 oz flour
1 egg
80 ml / 3 fl oz lager
oil for frying
cayenne pepper

Simmer the soft roes in salted water 3 minutes and drain them. Make a batter with the sifted flour, salt, egg and lager. Heat a pan of frying oil. Batter the roes and fry them a few at a time. Drain on absorbent paper, sprinkle with salt and dust with cayenne. Serve piping hot with pistou.

Soft Roes on Toast with Oyster Mushrooms and Hazelnut Oil

350 g / 12 oz oyster mushrooms
    (*pleurotes*)
4 tablespoons clarified butter
flour
450 g / 1 lb herring roes
4 slices wholemeal bread
salt
2 tablespoons hazelnut oil

Roughly chop the mushrooms. Divide the clarified butter between two pans. Flour the herring roes and fry them over a medium flame in one pan. Fry the mushrooms in the other pan over a high flame so that they colour at once. Toast the bread (with or without the crusts). Combine the mushrooms and soft roes. Season well. Pile them on toast and dribble hazelnut oil over the top.

NOTE: frozen herring roes are easily available, but they are rather mushy and may have an unpleasant fishy taste.

Sprat Escabeche

Marinating time 2 days
about 400 ml / 14 fl oz virgin
    olive oil
175 g / 6 oz finely sliced red
    onion
1 tablespoon chopped fresh
    thyme
1 bayleaf, cut into threads
1 clove garlic
sea salt
1 tablespoon diced red capsicum
1 tablespoon wine vinegar
flour (about 2 tablespoons)
700 g / 1½ lb sprats
oil for frying

Heat 1 tablespoon of olive oil in a pan, stew the onion and capsicum until soft, then add the herbs and let them cook for a couple of minutes more. Crush the garlic with sea salt and stir it into the pan. Add the wine vinegar. Remove from the heat.

Flour the sprats. Shallow fry them in oil and drain. Put them into a dish with the marinade. Pour over enough olive oil to immerse the sprats and leave them for a couple of days before eating.

Spider Crab and Olive Oil Sauce

Soak 2 anchovy fillets in water 30 minutes and drain. Put a live spider crab (preferably a hen) in a pan of cold salted water. The weight is not critical, something between 450–700 g / 1–1½ lb is fine. Bring to the boil. Allow to cool in the cooking liquid (keep the liquid for a soup, see page 25). Pick out all the meat. Pound it in a mortar with the anchovy until the meats are amalgamated though not completely smooth.

In a mixing bowl beat 3 egg yolks for a minute with a balloon whisk. Add a teaspoon of strong English mustard. Continue beating. Whisk in 120 ml / 4 fl oz of virgin olive oil, a few drops at a time, exactly as if you were starting off a mayonnaise. Then beat in the crab a little at a time. Season and add a squeeze of lemon juice. Whisk in a further 120 ml / 4 fl oz of olive oil. Adjust the seasoning.

Scrub out the spider crab's prickly carapace and fill with the sauce. Serve as a dip or as an accompaniment to a whole fish, or as part of a cold buffet.

Stuffed Fillets of Sole

150 g / 5 oz whiting fillet
30 g / 1 oz onion
1 teaspoon green peppercorns
zest of ¼ orange, grated
salt, pepper
1 tablespoon white breadcrumbs
a little milk
2 tablespoons double cream, chilled
12 fillets of sole
oil for frying
rice flour or cornflour
2 eggs, beaten

Blend the whiting, onion, peppercorns, orange zest, salt and pepper to a purée. Soak the breadcrumbs in milk and squeeze out all excess moisture. Blend the bread with the whiting. Chill one hour and blend in the cream. Spread this fine forcemeat on the sole fillets. Roll them up so they look like barrels and secure them with cocktail sticks.

Heat a pan of frying oil. Dust the fillets with flour and dip them in beaten egg. Fry the sole, roughly four pieces at a time. Drain on absorbent paper and season. Serve with a fresh tomato sauce.

Fresh Tomato Sauce

Drop 250 g / 9 oz tomato in boiling water for 12 seconds and remove the skin. Sieve the flesh. Combine with 1 teaspoon tomato purée, ½ teaspoon sugar, 1 diced 'bird's eye' chilli and 50 g / 2 oz diced shallot. Refrigerate 2 hours, salt and fold in chopped coriander leaves to taste.

Whitebait in a Crunchy Batter

350 g / 12 oz self-raising flour
30 g / 1 oz cornflour
salt, pepper
1 tablespoon oil
80 ml / 3 fl oz iced water
oil for frying
350 g / 12 oz whitebait or sprats

Whitebait are small sprats which can be eaten whole. Frozen ones, although of acceptable quality, do not compare with those which come fresh from the sea and whose silvery skin is dappled in rainbow tints. If you have the opportunity to buy several pounds fresh off a boat (usually in autumn), sort out the bigger sprats and reserve the tiny ones to make fried whitebait.

Sift the flour and cornflour with salt and pepper. Make into a batter by adding the oil and iced water.

Heat a pan of frying oil, or better still, put about 5 cups of oil in a wok. Coat the whitebait in this rather tacky batter. Fry them, a few at a time, until they are golden and crisp. Drain on absorbent paper and season. Serve them as a pre-dinner snack with pineapple cubes.

Fried Parsley and Fried Celery

Fried parsley was once considered an appropriate garnish for all fried fish dishes, though why is a mystery. Robert Courtine, who has ruled over French gastronomy for the last 20 years, serves it as a vegetable.

Another famous French food expert, the chef Alain Chapel, sometimes serves fried celery leaves with an apéritif. Instead of serving either with fried fish, try them with grilled mackerel or red mullet or even with a sauced dish which contains plenty of aromatic herbs and spices (not a cream sauce).

Heat your pan of frying oil, but take out the basket. Prepare sprigs of parsley or celery (coriander is worth trying too) which must be thoroughly dried. Put a few of them into the frying basket. Dip it into the hot oil. There is a sudden crackle as the leaves dry. Quickly lift out the basket. The parsley should still be green; it should be crisp and unshrivelled. Drain the leaves on absorbent paper and begin again. Do not worry if the leaves burn at the beginning while you are getting the knack. Just throw them out and start again. Once you have done it, it is like riding a bicycle, you don't forget.

NOTE: if you have some spare batter, scrub the roots of very fresh spring onions or leeks, dip them in batter and fry them.

75

Papillotes, Paupiettes and Lorgnettes

Lobster

The sight of a dish containing a finely garnished and tastefully presented turbot can be flattering to the host, but this should not be at the expense of quality. Mere appearance does not compensate for the deterioration in quality of food served half-cold.

From a recipe, *Turbot Braisé*, in
Le Guide Culinaire by Auguste Escoffier

Two basic techniques survive as the core of classical French fish cookery: poaching fish in a minimum of liquid and frying à la meunière.

By the first method, fish, typically a fillet or a small cut, is settled in a buttered pan of similar size with a little added stock, preferably hot. It is covered and set to cook in the oven for a few minutes, being basted once or twice to ensure that the top does not dry out. Once it is ready, the fish is drained and arranged on the silver flat. The stock and juices in the pan, sometimes with extra wine or stock, are reduced almost to a glaze, cream is whisked in and boiled until it coats the back of a spoon. Sometimes the sauce is enriched with egg yolk or butter or a combination of both.

Meunière takes its name from the eponymous miller's wife. Just before pan-frying, the fish is dusted with flour. It goes into a pan of hot, clarified butter and is cooked at the rate of about 10 minutes per inch of thickness at the broadest point. It is placed on the service dish, a little lemon juice is squeezed over it and some roughly chopped parsley sprinkled on top. At the very last moment before service, *beurre noisette*, brown butter, is poured over the fish 'so that the bubbling produced by the contact of the hot butter on the moist parsley is still discernible when the dish is presented to the guest'.

Both techniques have survived; both are popular wherever French cookery is practised seriously. But for how long? The war on butter, orchestrated presumably by margarine manufacturers, is reshaping cooking, and the use of steam has already started to replace both preparations in the opera houses of the cooking divas.

It is hard to assess how many of the classical skills have been dropped from current practice. Many fish which were rated highly at the turn of the century have all but vanished from the table: eel, carp, tench, pike, char, grayling, perch, sturgeon, smelts. Even the tasty brown trout has been ousted by the farmed rainbow trout.

Crimped fish, a peculiar English contribution to the classical canon, is lost but not regretted as a technique. It was supposed to firm up the flesh; the method smacks of barbarity. A live cod or salmon had deep gashes incised into its flesh from head to tail; it was soaked in water and then plunged into boiling salted water till it was just cooked.

Papillote cookery was the acme of fashion at the Savoy during the Ritz-Escoffier reign. Fish was wrapped in buttered greaseproof paper and baked to retain its natural juices. When we wrap a trout into a sheet of foil or, heaven forbid, bake a broiler-house chicken in a roasting bag, we merely echo the older ways.

Papillote cookery is regaining some of its prominence with the emergence of *sous vide* cookery, one of the newer stabs at food preservation. The proper title is *la cuisson en papillote sous vide*. A product, fish, flesh or vegetable, or a combination, is vacuum-sealed in a strengthened plastic pouch, steamed, chilled and stored until required when it can be reheated either by steam or as a boil-in-the-bag dish. The results are better than with frozen food, but only as good as the practitioner who prepares them.

The repertoire of classical dishes is dotted with technical terms to describe precise ways of cutting, folding or pressing pieces of fish: darnes, tronçons, épigrammes, médallions, gréadins and ondines, to name a few. The best-loved of the fancy shapes was the paupiette. Fillets of anything from anchovies to soles, usually coated in a thin layer of stuffing, are rolled up like a swiss roll. The variations are countless. For Sardines à la niçoise, pairs of sardine fillets are curled around a mushroom *duxelles* and tucked up in courgette flowers—a kind of floral papillote. In Filets de sole à l'andalouse, a sole paupiette surmounts a risotto-filled tomato or in Filets de sole Daumont, a mushroom covered in chopped crayfish.

The paupiette to end them all is the Lorgnette de merlan. Whiting fillets are skinned and detached from either side of the backbone, but left attached to the head. They are then thoroughly coated in egg and breadcrumbs. The fillets are rolled up along either side of the head and fastened with a skewer to resemble a pair of specs on the end of a pointed nose. The fish is then fried and served with tomato sauce.

As a spurious sophistication it is only a shade less outrageous than another whiting speciality, Merlan en colère (angry whiting), where the body is curled round towards the head so that the poor fish can bite its own tail. Thus arranged it is impossible to fry the whiting so that the concertinaed body cooks without overcooking the tail end.

Fumet de Poisson for Classic Sauces

250 g / 9 oz onions
parsley stalks
115 g / 4 oz mushrooms
2.25 kg / 5 lb fish trimmings
   (lemon sole, sole, turbot,
   brill, whiting or John Dory)
½ lemon
5 litres / 9 pints water
300 ml / ½ pint dry white wine
1 teaspoon black peppercorns
salt

Chop up the onions and a handful of parsley stalks with the mushrooms. Cover the bottom of a saucepan with vegetables and put the fish trimmings on top. Squeeze lemon juice over them. Add the water and bring to the boil. Skim away the scum which floats to the surface and add the wine. Simmer 20 minutes, add the peppercorns and simmer 10 minutes more. (You can add a pinch of salt but no more because the stock will be further reduced in any sauce and its flavour is going to be more concentrated.) Strain the fumet into a bowl.

Escoffier wrote: 'The use of inferior quality white wine will cause the stock to go a grey colour and it is far better to omit the wine altogether rather than use one of doubtful quality.'

NOTE: the mushrooms must be very fresh and white or they will discolour the stock. You may freeze some of the stock, but this tends to break down some of its gelatinous texture, although the flavour is unaffected.

Sauce au Vin Blanc

80 ml / 3 fl oz fumet made with
   wine (above)
1 tablespoon dry white wine
3 egg yolks
220 g / 8 oz unsalted butter
salt, pepper

There are two classic ways for preparing a white wine sauce. The first is to reduce the fumet with the extra wine until it forms a sticky film on the bottom of the pan. Cool 10 minutes and beat in the egg yolks. Transfer the mixture to a bowl over a pan of simmering water. Whisk the cubed butter into the yolks a few lumps at a time until it forms a warm emulsion. Season.

The second way is to reduce the fumet as before and

reserve. Put the eggs in a bowl over a pan of simmering water. Whisk in the butter as before and finally add the fumet. Adjust the seasoning.

As a modern alternative, blend the eggs in a liquidizer and dribble in the hot reduced fumet and wine. Melt the butter in a saucepan without boiling it and pour it hot, a little at a time on to the eggs while the liquidizer is rotating at a medium speed. Adjust the seasoning.

Paupiettes de Sole

For the farce:
115 g / 4 oz white fish (whiting, ling, salmon, seatrout, etc.)
nutmeg
½ teaspoon chopped shallot
salt, pepper
1 tablespoon egg white
150 ml / ¼ pint double cream

12 fillets of sole
salt, pepper
1 finely chopped shallot
120 g / 4½ oz butter
80 ml / 3 fl oz fumet
80 ml / 3 fl oz dry white wine
400 ml / 14 fl oz double cream

Put the fish for the farce in a food processor with a pinch of nutmeg, shallot, salt and pepper. Blend to a purée. Add the egg white and blend again. Chill the mixture for one hour. Add cream and blend once more. This is enough for 24 fillets, but the mixture will freeze.

Flatten and season the skinned fillets. Spread an even layer of farce on the flat side of the fillets and roll them up to form roughly barrel-shaped paupiettes.

Sprinkle shallot in a buttered ovenproof dish. Place the fillets on top and pour over the fumet and white wine. Brush the top of the paupiettes with 40 g / 1½ oz melted butter. Cover the dish with foil and bake at 220°C, 425°F, gas mark 7, until the stuffing has set, about 12 minutes. Drain the paupiettes and arrange them on four hot plates. Reduce the liquid in the dish. Add the cream and reduce to a coating consistency. Beat the rest of the butter into the sauce. Whisk it using a zigzag stroke, to give it a fine gloss. Check the seasoning and pour over the paupiettes.

Paupiettes de Sole à la Crème d'Oursins

12 paupiettes de sole (see preceding recipe)
15 g / ½ oz butter
80 ml / 3 fl oz fumet
80 ml / 3 fl oz dry white wine
16 prawns
200 ml / 7 fl oz hollandaise sauce
115 g / 4 oz sea urchin

Not all French classic recipes at the beginning of the 20th century appeared in *Le Guide Culinaire*, but it influenced the way cooks interpreted regional cooking. This recipe follows quite closely one which appeared in the sixth edition of *La Cuisinière Provençale* (1895).

Prepare the uncooked paupiettes as described in the preceding recipe. Lay them in a buttered dish with

79

fumet and wine. Cover and bake 12 minutes in a hot oven at 220°C, 425°F, gas mark 7. Arrange in a circle on four hot plates. Fill each one with 4 shelled prawns. Reduce the cooking liquid and beat it into the hollandaise sauce. Holding the sea urchin firmly in a teatowel, remove the top with a sharp knife, scoop out the orange roe. Purée roe and fold into the sauce. Spoon over the paupiettes.

Hollandaise Sauce c. 1895

'Melt a lump of butter the size of a walnut in a pan and add a spoon of flour. Moisten with a glass of water and stir to prevent lumps forming. Do not let it boil, it should be thickish. Beat in two yolks and then, little by little, two ounces of butter. Season and add a little lemon juice.'

Hollandaise Sauce

Stand a bowl over a pan of simmering water. Put 3 yolks and a tablespoon of water in the bowl. Season and whisk until smooth. Beat 220 g / 8 oz of warmed butter into the sauce a little at a time to obtain a thick, emulsified sauce. Beat in lemon juice.

Consommé de Poisson

115 g / 4 oz diced leek
30 g / 1 oz chopped onion
½ bayleaf
50 g / 2 oz chopped parsley and celery leaves
1 kg / 2¼ lb fish bones, heads and trimmings (turbot, brill, sole, John Dory)
2 litres / 3½ pints water
300 ml / ½ pint dry white wine

If concentrated fumets were used for sauces, fish consommé was preferred by classic chefs for making soups.

Put the leek, onion, bayleaf, parsley and celery in a pan. Add the fish bones and trimmings. Pour over the water and wine. Boil, skim, add a cup of cold water, simmer 45 minutes and strain through a fine sieve.

Bisque de Homard

115 g / 4 oz Carolina rice
1.5 litres / 2½ pints fish consommé

Simmer the rice 40 minutes in fish consommé and set aside. Fry the carrot and onion in 50 g / 2 oz butter until they start to brown. Add thyme, parsley stalks and

50 g / 2 oz diced carrot
50 g / 2 oz chopped onion
150 g / 5 oz butter
sprig of thyme
3 parsley stalks
1 dried bayleaf
1 × 700 g / 1½ lb lobster
1 tablespoon brandy
115 ml / 4 fl oz dry white wine
80 ml / 3 fl oz double cream
salt, cayenne pepper

crumbled bayleaf. Stew for a minute. Chop up the lobster (page 37), add it to the pan and cook, turning the pieces often until the shell turns red. Turn up the heat, pour in the brandy and flame. Add the white wine and let it reduce. Add three-quarters of the fish consommé and simmer 10 minutes. Take out the pieces of lobster tail. Remove the meat from the shell and claws and dice. Put the pieces of lobster shell and any other bits into a food processor a few pieces at a time. Liquidize these chopped bits with all the consommé including the rice and vegetables. Strain the liquid through a sieve or conical strainer. Whisk the cream and then the remaining butter into the soup. Season with salt and cayenne. Stir in the diced lobster and serve.

Rouget en Papillote

Serves 1
1 large red mullet
salt, pepper
40 g / 1½ oz butter
1 sprig rosemary, finely chopped
1 tablespoon lemon juice

At the turn of the century when papillote cookery was at its height, the fish was wrapped in buttered greaseproof paper, which puffed up when baked in the oven. Before greaseproof paper was invented a pig's bladder was used in the same way. Paul Bocuse still serves *poularde en vessie*, chicken in a bladder, at his restaurant outside Lyons. Foil has replaced greaseproof paper in a modern kitchen because it is more robust. It also deflects some of the heat and prevents overcooking. It has a further advantage in that liquid is sealed inside the foil package with no risk of it soaking through. The classic 'en papillote' recipes often specify a thick sauce to be spooned into the parcel along with the fish.

Cut out a piece of foil somewhat longer than the mullet and large enough to encase it. Season the mullet. Combine 30 g / 1 oz softened butter with the rosemary. Place inside the mullet. Brush the foil with the remaining melted butter and lay the fish on top. Squeeze lemon juice over it. Seal the fish in the foil package making pleats at the edges to prevent any moisture escaping. Bake 15–25 minutes at 190°C, 375°F, gas mark 5, depending on the size of the mullet.
    Open at the table with a sharp pair of scissors.
    This basic recipe can be varied in many different ways by changing the type or cut of fish and the flavourings.

Rougets Grillés Francillon

4 red mullet
65 ml / 2½ fl oz olive oil
30 ml / 1 fl oz lemon juice
4 slices bread
220 g / 8 oz unsalted butter
700 g / 1½ lb tomatoes
1 clove garlic
bouquet garni (thyme, bayleaf
   and parsley)
220 g / 8 oz waxy potatoes
oil for frying
salt, pepper
parsley with stalks
1 anchovy fillet

Classical kitchens never lacked for pairs of underpaid hands, and elements prepared in different corners of the kitchen were often brought together for the final service. Here, the *poissonier* would have prepared the fish, the *saucier* the sauce and the *chef rôtisseur* the *pommes paille*.

Scale the mullet and remove the gills but not the rest of the innards. Score the flesh on both sides. Marinate in 50 ml / 2 fl oz olive oil and the lemon juice for 30 minutes. Cut 4 slices of bread to act as beds for the grilled fish. Melt 80 g / 3 oz of butter, skim off the froth and strain the clarified butter into a clean frying pan. Fry the bread until golden.

Drop the tomatoes in boiling water 12 seconds, skin, halve and seed them. Rub a frying pan with garlic, brush it with oil, add the tomatoes and bouquet garni. Cover and stew gently for 40 minutes. Strain the sauce and reduce to 200 ml / ⅓ pint.

Shred the potatoes, wash and pat dry. Deep fry them till golden and sprinkle with salt. Deep fry the parsley (page 75). Rinse the anchovy, purée it with the remaining butter, beat it into the sauce and adjust the seasoning.

Grill the fish rapidly, basting it with the marinade. Season and serve on the fried bread garnished with potato straws, fried parsley and tomato sauce (there is more sauce here than is strictly necessary).

Sole Meunière

Serves 1
40 g / 1½ oz flour
salt, pepper
1 × 400 g / 14 oz sole
40 g / 1½ oz clarified butter

Literally speaking, sole meunière is done the miller's wife's way. Naturally she used some flour.

Sift the flour and season it. Dip the sole in flour and shake off any excess so it is just covered in a thin, powdery coat. Fry at once in hot clarified butter. If you leave the floured sole lying around it becomes tacky and unpleasant.

Many French cooks fry the sole in a pool of butter. When the fish is cooked, they brown extra butter—as though too much were not enough—and pour it over the fish at the last moment. From the health point of view that may sound like filling a hypodermic with a concentrated shot of cholesterol, but if you do it this way from time to time, you will not come to much harm. If you brush your pan with a neutral cooking oil, heat it and add a lump of butter before frying the fish, its flavour is as good.

Don't overcook sole. It should be opaque when cooked but still moist. Five minutes will probably be long enough.

Filets de Turbotin aux Ceps

1 × 1.35 kg / 3 lb turbot
450 g / 1 lb ceps (*boletus edulis*)
150 g / 5 oz butter
2 tablespoons olive oil
salt, pepper
flour
1 tablespoon chopped parsley
¼ lemon

Fillet the turbot and skin it. Cut out the spongy parts of the boletus caps if they are large. Trim the bottom of the stalks. Cut the ceps into thin slices. Melt ⅓ of the butter in a pan with the oil. Fry the ceps until they colour, then turn down the heat.

Dip the fillets in seasoned flour. Melt half the remaining butter in another pan and fry the turbot about 6 minutes. Drain the fish, transfer to four preheated plates and sprinkle chopped parsley over it. Squeeze some lemon juice over it. Wipe out the pan with kitchen paper and add the rest of the butter. When it sizzles pour it over the fillets and serve garnished with ceps.

Barbue sur le Plat

50 g / 2 oz butter
1 × 1.35 kg / 3 lb brill
salt, pepper
300 ml / ½ pint fumet (page 78)
1 tablespoon white wine
    (Chablis)

Brush a large baking tray with some melted butter. Scale the brill and trim away the fins with kitchen scissors. Lay it in the baking tray, black skin down. Cut down through the middle of the white side following the line of the backbone. Season and dot the fish with small lumps of butter. Pour the fumet and wine into the tray. Put in a very hot oven, 230°C, 450°F, gas mark 8 and bake until done, basting the fish every 2 minutes. By the time that it is cooked, the white skin will be coated in a glistening syrupy glaze. Transfer to a serving dish and serve without any sauce or garnish, except maybe some new potatoes and a salad.

83

Babyfood Syndrome

skate

Steam the hake four minutes and mash it. Add a few drops of lemon juice. Trim the stalks of the spinach and wash it in water with lemon juice added. Drain it and shred it finely. Chop the pine kernels. Combine the fish, spinach and yoghourt. Sprinkle pine kernels and sesame seeds over them.
Translated from *Recettes originales pour tout-petits*, by Eventhia Senderens

The VCM has a large stainless-steel bowl. In its centre are two scythe-like blades which revolve faster than the knives attached to Boudicca's chariot wheels. If you load a few pounds of fish in the bowl and switch on the motor, it takes no more than a few seconds to turn muscle into paste. Yes, the vertical cutting machine is the big daddy of modern food processors.

Around the mid-70s astute professional chefs discovered that this tool could produce one of the *gloires* of haute cuisine, quenelles, in a few shakes. The classic method involves pounding fish, usually pike, in a mortar, forcing it through a sieve, chilling it over ice and beating in double cream. The process takes an hour or so, depending on the quantity.

At about the same time, two crusading journalists, Henri Gault and Christian Millau, were squeezing the best part of the juice from their nouvelle cuisine fashion. Everything edible had to be lighter than air: light sauces, light soufflés, light mousses and mousselines, light purées, light boudins, light terrines.

For sound economic reasons it suited the professionals to drift with this vogue. A salmon mousseline cost them half as much as a salmon steak, and not much more effort. If it tasted bland, no matter; at least it was light. What was lacking could be supplied by the *sauciers'* savoir-faire.

Besides, it opened up unexploited areas in which they could show off their new technique. The basic fish mousse recipe combined a kilo of fish, two to four eggs and a kilo of cream. From this, chefs evolved terrines which were multi-coloured, multilayered, mottled, flecked and speckled. Some could be confused with a Battenburg cake. The word *gâteau*, as in *gâteau de foies blonds* or *gâteau de St Jacques* became current on French menus. Made to the same standard formula and with the same equipment, these creations were uniformly light and mostly bland.

It would not be hard to react cynically to these babyfood delicacies, if that was all they were. But the critics who had the most to say against them would be happy to tuck into bangers and mash, the pork chopped to a pulp in a similar machine, probably with crushed ice, the potato punched to a shapeless wad of flavoured starch.

Sausages, depending on what you put in them, can either be a good excuse for turning vegetarian, or for vegans to revert to being omnivores. Mash, with the help of salt and pepper mills, cream and butter, is a delicacy. So it is unfair to decry any fish recipe which does not arrive at the table looking unmistakably like the fish it came from. Nor is there any reason why the texture should resemble tofu. Chinese fish balls are almost rubbery between the teeth. Potted and other fish pastes of the kipper pâté type have a coarse texture, or can do. The standard mousseline recipe will be fluffier when poached in stock or soup than when steamed. Cooked and allowed to go cold in a terrine, it is firm enough to slice.

Nor need the taste be monotonous. A little nutmeg or mace in a salmon mousse, vermouth with sole or whiting, basil with scallops, horseradish with smoked fish are just four obvious suggestions of how to boost the flavour. Gourmets concerned about food aesthetics who have reacted to messy mixtures argue that every individual flavour on the plate should be recognizable. Often they may be right, but subtle or even aggressive blending also has its place, witness the English sausage.

The *Cook's Manual* by Meg Dods, an early 19th-century Scottish cookery book, has a dish described as Teased Skate. The wing is first boiled, then baked until the bones can be pulled out easily. 'The flesh,' states the recipe, 'being now detached from the bones, it should be put into cloth and well rubbed with the hands till it puts on a woolly appearance, which it will soon do.' The teased fish is then stirred into half a pound of butter and eaten with egg sauce and mashed parsnips. Messrs Gault and Millau would probably approve. Cooks are infinitely ingenious. Whatever trick is possible, sooner or later someone will try it. There is no harm in turning prime fish into pap, only in doing so once too often.

Capsicum and Avocado Mousses with Crabmeat

4 leaves gelatine
300 g / 10 oz avocado
1 teaspoon grated onion
½ lime
1 sprig coriander
salt, pepper, cayenne pepper
450 g / 1 lb red capsicums
115 g / 4 oz onion
1 tablespoon groundnut oil
1 pinch strong paprika
50 ml / 2 fl oz simmering water
175 g / 6 oz white crabmeat
300 ml / ½ pint double cream
1 egg white
cucumber and tomato to garnish

Soak the gelatine in water. Blend the avocado to a purée with the grated onion, lime juice, coriander and seasoning. Dice the capsicum and onion. Stew them in oil until soft, add paprika, salt and cayenne and blend to a purée.

Dissolve the gelatine in the simmering water. Divide the crabmeat between the two purées. Mix the gelatine into the two purées. Whip the cream and egg white together until it holds its shape on the whisk. Divide the cream equally and fold into each purée. Pour one mousse into a glass bowl, smooth its surface and put in the freezer for 15 minutes. Remove and cover with the second mousse. Transfer to the fridge and leave to set.

Decorate with cucumber and tomatoes.

Fish Cakes

40 g / 1½ oz butter
115 g / 4 oz diced onion
1 heaped tablespoon flour
250 ml / 9 fl oz milk
2 yolks
1 tablespoon chopped parsley
salt, pepper
450 g / 1 lb cooked white fish
   (seatrout, cod, whiting, hake)
flour, egg and breadcrumbs for
   coating
50 ml / 2 fl oz oil
50 g / 2 oz butter

Fish cakes often taste, as well as look, like fried hockey pucks. They are probably made with four parts old mashed potato to one part of old fish. There is another way.

Melt the butter in a pan and cook the onion until softened. Stir in flour and let it cook for 2 minutes without colouring. Add hot milk to make a thick sauce. Cook 10 minutes. Cool and beat in the egg yolks. Add parsley and season heavily. Fold in the flaked, cooked fish. Chill the mixture, then divide it into 12 on a floured work surface. Roll each lump into a disc. Dip in beaten egg and breadcrumbs. Fry the fishcakes in a mixture of oil and butter.

Fillets of Brill with Nettle and Sorrel Mousse

220 g / 8 oz sorrel
115 g / 4 oz nettle tops
1 × 1.35 kg / 3 lb brill
salt
150 ml / ¼ pint double cream
4 egg yolks
50 g / 2 oz butter

Pull out the sorrel stalks. Drop the leaves and nettles in a pan of boiling salted water. Drain after one minute and chop with a stainless steel knife. Put in a sieve and press out any excess moisture.

Fillet and skin the brill. Season the fillets and steam them over a pan of boiling water (or one containing an infusion of seaweed).

Put the sorrel and nettles in an enamel or stainless steel pan with the cream. Bring to the boil and take off the heat. Beat in the yolks with a wooden spoon and then add the butter a few lumps at a time. Check the seasoning (no pepper).

Spoon the sauce, which should be more than tepid, but not quite hot, on to four plates with the fillets on top of them.

NOTE: always use enamel or stainless steel utensils when cooking sorrel.

Monkfish Puddings with Crab

Serves 6
50 g / 2 oz white of leek
20 g / ⅔ oz butter
2 slices white bread
milk
220 g / 8 oz monkfish
2 egg whites
salt, white pepper
250 ml / 9 fl oz double cream, chilled
115 g / 4 oz crabmeat

For the sauce:
30 g / 1 oz dried morels, soaked in advance
1 tablespoon dry vermouth
200 ml / 7 fl oz double cream
salt, pepper

Dice the leek and stew it gently in butter. Cool. Soak the bread in milk and squeeze out the excess moisture. Chill. Blend the leek, bread and monkfish in a food processor. Add egg whites, salt and pepper and blend again. Chill the purée 1 hour, add the chilled cream and blend again. Fold the crabmeat into the mixture.

Fill six buttered ramekins with the mixture. Cover each one with a circle of buttered greaseproof paper. Stand the ramekins in a tray containing simmering water which comes half way up their sides. Bake 15–20 minutes in a moderate oven, 180°C, 350°F, gas mark 4.

Boil the morels in the water in which they soaked, for 25 minutes, then remove with a slotted spoon. Add vermouth to the liquid and reduce it to a glaze. Add 200 ml / 7 fl oz cream and boil until reduced to a light sauce. Return the morels to the pan and heat through. Check the seasoning. Turn out the crab puddings and pour sauce round them.

Haddock and Mash Fritters

350 g / 12 oz potatoes
salt, pepper
2 tablespoons chopped chives
1 egg, beaten
2 tablespoons grated Cheddar
350 g / 12 oz smoked haddock
300 ml / ½ pint milk
flour, egg and breadcrumbs for
    coating
2 beef tomatoes
½ large red onion
2 cloves garlic, finely chopped
1 tablespoon chopped tarragon
2 tablespoons olive oil
oil for frying

Peel the potatoes, boil them in salted water and mash by hand. Don't mind the odd lump. Add chives, egg and cheese. Season.

Poach the haddock in milk. Drain, flake and mix with the potato. Prepare trays of flour, egg and crumbs for coating.

Slice the tomatoes and onion, combine with garlic and tarragon. Pour over olive oil and season.

Heat a pan of frying oil or put 5 cups of oil in a wok. Roll haddock and potato nuggets in flour, egg and breadcrumbs. Fry till golden, drain on absorbent paper, sprinkle with salt and serve on the bed of tomatoes and onion.

Potted Crab Sippets

115 g / 4 oz white crabmeat
1 tablespoon brown crabmeat
175 g / 6 oz butter
1 pinch mace
1 dash Tabasco
1 teaspoon Amontillado sherry
white bread

Mash the crabmeats together with 115 g / 4 oz softened butter, mace, Tabasco and sherry. Put in a large ramekin or similar stoneware dish. Press down and smooth the surface. Put the remaining butter in a small pan, bring to the boil and skim off the froth on the surface. Let the sediment settle. Spoon this clarified butter over the potted crab.

To make sippets, slice the white bread thinly and cut off the crusts. Toast the slices and cut each one into eight triangles. Spread the potted crab on the toast and serve as canapés or hors d'oeuvre.

Potted Smoked Haddock

300 g / 10 oz Finnan haddock
300 ml / ½ pint milk
300 ml / ½ pint double cream
salt, pepper
clarified butter

Poach the haddock in the milk and discard bones and skin. Fork through the flesh till it forms a fluffy mass. Beat in the cream and season. Put the fish in a sieve and let it drain for 4 hours. Turn the fish into ramekins and press down. Cover with clarified butter and serve with toast.

Poached Mousselines of Seatrout

220 g / 8 oz seatrout fillet
1 pinch mace
salt, white pepper
2 egg whites
250 ml / 9 fl oz double cream,
  chilled

For the sauce:
115 ml / 4 fl oz fumet (page 78)
115 ml / 4 fl oz dry white wine
300 ml / ½ pint double cream,
  chilled
1 teaspoon Chambéry or dry
  vermouth
chopped chives to garnish

Theoretically, quenelles contain flour and mousselines don't. Practically, they are almost identical twins. You will notice more difference between a poached mousseline and a steamed one. The poached version is fluffier, especially if it is made with small pieces. Ideally you want a straight, shallow-sided pan at least 30 cm / 12 inches across. Whatever the diameter cut out two circles of non-stick baking parchment slightly smaller than the pan.

Chop up the seatrout. Blend it to a paste in a food processor. Add mace, half a teaspoon of salt, white pepper and egg whites and blend again. Chill the mixture for 1 hour, incorporate the cream and blend again.

Mould the mousselines into lozenges with two dessertspoons. Arrange them on the sheets of parchment, leaving space between them to allow for swelling. Drop the sheets into the pan of gently boiling water and cook 5 minutes. Drain the mousselines one by one with a slotted spoon.

Mousselines shrink like soufflés, so start on the sauce before you poach them. Reduce the fumet and the wine by half. Add the cream to the fumet and reduce to a coating consistency. Whisk in the Chambéry and season. Coat the mousselines with sauce and garnish with chives.

Skate and Smoked Salmon Rillettes

1 × 700 g / 1½ lb skate wing
1.2 litres / 2 pints water
50 ml / 2 fl oz vinegar
175 g / 6 oz smoked salmon
115 g / 4 oz softened butter
80 ml / 3 fl oz double cream
¼ lemon
salt, pepper

Put the skate wing in a roasting tin, pour over water and vinegar, cover with foil and bake 20–25 minutes at 200°C, 400°F, gas mark 6. Drain, scrape off the white skin and cool slightly.

Cut the smoked salmon in thin strips about the diameter of spaghetti. Fillet the cooked skate while still warm and flake it. Combine the butter, cream, lemon juice, salt and pepper. The mixture should have the texture of creamed fat. Fold in the skate and salmon and leave to set overnight. Serve with hot toast.

Sautéed Dogfish with a Purée of Baby Turnips and Garlic

700 g / 1½ lb baby turnips
7 g / ¼ oz garlic cloves
salt, pepper
2 level teaspoons sugar
50 g / 2 oz unsalted butter for
  glazing
2 egg yolks
40 ml / 1½ fl oz milk or cream
1 tablespoon chopped parsley
2 tablespoons flour
700 g / 1½ lb dogfish (huss)
30 g / 1 oz butter
50 ml / 2 fl oz groundnut oil
¼ lemon

Turnips have always been scorned in the West Country, presumably because the poor ate them when they were large and unappetizing. The Devonshire saying, 'She has given him turnips' means that a lass rejected the advances of a suitor.

Peel and quarter the turnips. Peel the garlic cloves. Put them in a pan with just enough water to cover. Add salt and simmer 5 minutes. Discard half the water, add sugar and the unsalted butter. Boil hard until the water has evaporated and the turnips glazed. Cool slightly, blend in a food processor with the egg yolks and thin out with cream.

Combine parsley and flour. Cut the dogfish into 2.5 cm / 1 inch steaks. Heat the butter and the oil in a pan. Dust the fish with flour and fry rapidly. Squeeze lemon juice over it. Serve the fish with the purée.

Smoked Salmon Terrine

Serves 12
4 leaves gelatine
150 ml / ¼ pint simmering
  water
115 g / 4 oz finely sliced smoked
  salmon for lining the terrine
150 g / 5 oz smoked salmon
1 teaspoon tomato purée
1½ tablespoons lemon juice
salt, pepper
600 ml / 1 pint double cream
30 g / 1 oz horseradish
40 g / 1½ oz watercress
150 g / 5 oz skinned Arbroath
  smokie

Soak the gelatine in cold water for 30 minutes. Meanwhile, chill a 2 litre / 3½ pint terrine in the freezer. Drain the gelatine and dissolve it in hot water. Line the terrine with smoked salmon slices, dipped in the gelatine solution. The cold terrine makes them stick like wallpaper. Slices should overlap the edges, so that they can be folded back. You should still have a few tablespoons of gelatine solution left after dipping the smoked salmon.

Blend 150 g / 5 oz smoked salmon, tomato purée, half the lemon juice and 4 teaspoons of gelatine solution. Add a little salt and plenty of pepper. Fold in 150 ml / ¼ pint cream, whisked until stiff. Spread the mixture on the bottom of the terrine and put in the fridge while you attack the second mousse.

Grate the horseradish (wear goggles if you don't want sore eyes). Chop the cress. Fold it into 150 ml / ¼ pint whipped cream with the horseradish, 4 teaspoons gelatine solution, the remaining lemon juice, salt and pepper. Spread the mixture on the smoked salmon layer and return to the fridge.

Purée the Arbroath smokie with 90 ml / 3 fl oz cream. Add 4 teaspoons gelatine solution and a little salt. Fold in the remaining whipped cream. Spread the final mousse layer on the terrine. Turn over the smoked salmon flaps to cover, and leave to set for about 4 hours before turning out.

Steamed Lemon Sole, Mashed Swede and Maltaise Sauce

450 g / 1 lb swede
30 g / 1 oz butter
40 ml / 1½ fl oz milk
1 blood orange
1 yolk
80 g / 3 oz chilled unsalted
   butter
salt, pepper
¼ lemon
4 lemon soles
seaweed

Classic recipes insist on blood oranges for maltaise sauce, but it's rare to find ones dark enough to affect the sauce's colour. However, blood oranges are quite sharp and this is what gives the sauce its characteristic bite.

Peel and chop the swede, boil in salted water until tender, drain and mash with butter and milk. Beat in the juice of half a blood orange and keep hot.

Put a bowl over a pan of simmering water. Put the egg yolk in it with a teaspoon of blood orange juice and beat for half a minute. Whisk in cubes of the chilled butter, a few at a time, adding the remaining orange juice intermittently. When the sauce has formed a warm emulsion, season and finish with a dash of lemon juice. Give an energetic whisk so that it becomes light and frothy.

Roll up the skinned, seasoned lemon sole fillets and steam them on a bed of seaweed. Drain on absorbent paper. Spoon mashed swede on to dinner plates, arrange fillets on top and coat them with sauce.

Steamed Whiting Mousseline with Cashew Nuts and Mint Sauce

175 g / 6 oz whiting fillet
1 egg white
1 scrape of nutmeg
salt
175 ml / 6 fl oz double cream, chilled
seaweed

For the sauce:
30 g / 1 oz finely diced onion
30 g / 1 oz butter
1½ tablespoons white wine vinegar
1 tablespoon finely chopped mint
115 ml / 4 fl oz double cream
50 g / 2 oz cashew nuts to garnish
salt, pepper

Put the whiting fillet in the freezer 40 minutes. Blend it to a purée, add the egg white, nutmeg and salt and blend again. Chill 1 hour and blend in the very cold double cream. Refrigerate the cold mousseline base.

Brush four ramekins with butter, fill them with mousseline, pressing the mixture well down with the back of a spoon. Put a layer of fresh seaweed in the bottom of a pan and cover with water. Stand the mousselines on a rack over the seaweed. Bring the water to the boil, cover the pan and steam for 15 minutes until the mousselines have set.

While they are cooking, sweat the onion in butter, pour over the vinegar and reduce to a glaze. Stir in the mint. Add the cream and shake the pan back and forth until it is hot and lightly thickened. Check the seasoning. Toast the cashew nuts.

Turn out the contents of the ramekins on to four plates, spoon over the sauce and garnish with freshly toasted cashews.

Fish in a Coffin

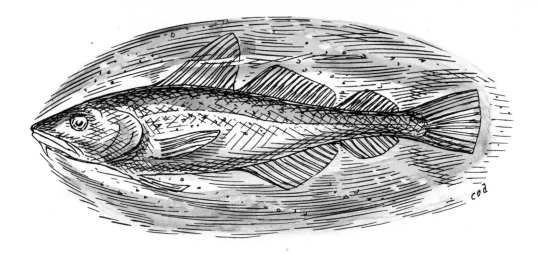

Here, into the dust,
The mouldering crust
Of Elenor Batchelour's shoven;
Well vers'd in the arts
Of pies, custards, and tarts
And the lucrative skill of the oven

When she'd lived long enough
She made her last puff—
A puff by her husband much prais'd:
Now here she doth lie
And makes a dirt pie
In hope that her crust *shall be* rais'd.

To the pye-house Memory of Nell Batchelour,
the Oxford Pye-woman

John Murrell's recipe for tench baked in pastry is almost identical to a famous dish, *loup en croûte*, of a modern chef. The biggest difference is that Murrell was writing about 1620, whereas Paul Bocuse serves his speciality at Collonges-au-Mont-d'Or in the late 20th century.

'To bake a tench with a pudding in her belly,' described the Englishman, 'let your fish bled in the taile, then scalde it and scowre it: wash it cleane and drye it with a cloath. Then take grated bread, sweet creame, the yolkes of two or three new-laid egges, a few parboiled currans, a few sweet hearbs chopt fine. Season it with nutmeg and pepper and make it into a stiff pudding and put it into your tenches belly. Season your fish on the outside with a little pepper, salt and nutmeg and so put him in a deep coffin with a piece of sweet butter and so close your pye and bake it. Then take it out of the oven and open it and cast in a piece of a preserved orange. Then take vinegar, nutmeg, butter, sugar and the yolk of a new laid egge and boyle it on a chaffingdish of coales always stirring it to keep it from curdling. Then pour it into your pye, shogge [shake] it well together and serve it in.'

Chez Bocuse, à waiter lifts the lid off the fish-shaped pie to reveal the bass stuffed with a fish mousseline. He transfers a portion to the customer's plate, spoons hollandaise or Choron sauce over it and replaces a piece of the lid on top.

Pastry has always formed an essential part of the British culinary heritage. Depending on the fingers through which it passes and the purpose it is intended to serve, it can be either a crusty armour, an insubstantial negligé or any of a dozen different textures betwixt and between. Nearly all have their place. The thick hides of huff paste protected the dry haunches of venison as they turned on the spits of our forebears. The creamy inside of a raised pie absorbs the jelly and the fat in a meaty pork pie. Firm but melting short paste supplies the edible packaging of a Devonshire split or a Cornish pasty. Feathery puff pastry mops up the subtlest sauce.

Why then should fish pie, along with shepherd's pie and cottage pie, be made with a potato topping? At the end of the 18th century, the English working classes began the shift in diet which, on the one hand reduced the amount of bread and cereals they ate, and on the other filled the vacuum with potatoes.

The well-intentioned but pontificating Dr William Buchan typified fashionable medical opinion. 'Bread,' he wrote, 'made with butter is almost indigestible and pastries of every kind are little better; yet many people live on pastry and it is universally given to children. It is little better, however, than poison and never fails to disorder their stomachs.' (*Observations concerning the Diet of the Common People*.) So it was that instead of burying their fish in pastry, housewives began piling a burial mound of potato on top of it.

Some fish pies which disappeared from our national repertoire as the direct result of growing potato power need not be regretted. Stargazey pie, which has pilchard heads poking their noses out of the rim of a pastry lid, still appeals to art directors who specialize in food photography, but few, if any, cooks will ever attempt the recipe. In any case, pilchard shoals have long deserted the Cornish coast. Eel Island pie is virtually a lost dish because nobody fancies impaling a live eel.

Having watched the common people playing hide and seek with a fish and a potato, the Victorian middle classes decided to join in. In *The Cookery of England* Elisabeth Ayrton records a recipe for sole in a coffin where a fillet of sole is entombed in a scooped out jacket potato. 'Filets de sole Otéro' (named after the famous courtesan) is a classical look-alike; fish, shrimp and cheese sauce are pumped into a potato and glazed.

By the Edwardian era vol-au-vent, a puff pastry coffin with a small lid, had come into vogue, and these are still served today, typically on cruise liners or at chi-chi buffets. They are claimed to have been an invention of Antonin Carême, who had worked for the Prince Regent a century earlier. He is said to have left the future George IV, because the latter, despite his great size, showed no discrimination in eating.

Freshly made, a vol-au-vent is hot, flaky and filled with a rich sauce containing a salpicon of chicken, lobster or prawns. More often, nowadays, the pastry is stale and it contains a cold, flavoured glue. This deserves to be buried.

Puff Pastry

115 g / 4 oz softened unsalted butter
450 g / 1 lb plain, all purpose flour
350 g / 12 oz cold unsalted butter
1 teaspoon salt
175–200 ml / 6–7 fl oz cold water
(extra flour)

Every hypermarket, supermarket and delicatessen stocks puff pastry and few of us still bother to make it, which is a pity. The commercial variety rises like a dream, but it is not melting like good puff pastry should be and the taste is modest, to say the least.

There was a time when every cookery book had its puff paste recipe (there are at least three variants on how to make it). What they fail to do is give the *feel* of the paste, which is every bit as important as the method. They also concentrate on the time-consuming aspect, as though it were a chore. On the contrary, it is satisfying to make, like kneading bread. Try making it during an evening's television watching whilst the advertisements are showing.

You need to work in a cool kitchen—sub 18°C, 65°F is vital.

Rub the softened butter into the flour. Pound the hard butter to form a rectangle roughly 15 × 10 cm / 6 × 4 inches. Dissolve the salt in the water.

Add the water to the flour and knead it till it forms a silky elastic ball. This will take 10–15 minutes. Cover the paste with a cloth and leave it for 20 minutes or so. Flour a cool work surface. Roll out the dough to form a rectangle roughly 30 × 23 cm / 12 × 9 inches. Lay the slab of butter bang in the middle of it. Fold the edges of paste into the centre so as to completely enfold the butter. Roll out the pastry again. It is very tempting to squeeze the pastry by pressing the pin hard on to it, but don't. Fold the pastry into three, and give it a 20 minute rest.

That first rolling must be repeated 6 times. After each roll and fold, turn it through 90°; this is known as a 'turn'. If you find that lumps of butter are starting to seep through the paste, you either did not knead the dough enough in the first place, or the butter is too hard, or the room too warm, or someone is being too heavy-handed with the rolling pin. Although it is necessary to roll on a floured surface, try not to roll extra flour into the paste. The best thing is to brush the rectangle after each turn.

Bouchées and Vol-au-Vent

These classic pastry cases made with puff pastry are different from each other only in regard to size. To make a vol-au-vent you will need a 7.5 cm / 3 inch diameter pastry cutter or even a 10 cm / 4 inch one. For bouchées a 4 cm / 1½ inch one is right. Bear in mind that the puff pastry shrinks during baking.

To prepare six vol-au-vent you will need 350 g / 12 oz of prepared puff paste, a little beaten egg, a good baking sheet and some water. In addition, you will require a 7.5 cm / 3 inch and a 5 cm / 2 inch cutter.

Roll out the pastry thinly enough to cut out 12 circles with the larger cutter. Brush the baking sheet with water and lay six circles on it.

Take the small cutter and stamp an inner ring on to the remaining large circles. Lightly water the circles already on the sheet and lay the other six on top of them. Press down lightly. Brush the tops with beaten egg; be careful that the egg does not dribble on to the sides, which would stop the puff pastry from rising.

Bake 12–15 minutes in a very hot oven, 230°C, 450°F, gas mark 8 until well risen and golden on top. Take out of the oven.

Cut around the inner rings and remove the gilded centres. Take a pointed teaspoon or coffee spoon and scoop any uncooked pastry out of the middle. Discard it. Return the vol-au-vent to the oven for 5 minutes.

To prepare 24–30 bouchées, proceed exactly as for vol-au-vent, but use 4 cm / 1½ inch and 2.5 cm / 1 inch cutters. Bake for a slightly shorter time.

Cod's Roe Bouchées

150 g / 5 oz smoked cod's roe
4 slices crustless white bread
a little milk
50 g / 2 oz melted unsalted
　butter
100 ml / 3½ fl oz double cream
3 cloves garlic, chopped
60 puff pastry bouchées
lemon juice (optional)

Soak the cod's roe 20 minutes and scrape out the contents from the skin which encases it. Soak the bread in milk and squeeze out the excess moisture. Liquidize the roe, bread, butter, cream and garlic. You can add lemon juice if you want to.

Spoon the filling into the bouchées and serve as canapés.

Mussel and Salsify Vol-au-Vent

Serves 6
220 g / 8 oz salsify
1 teaspoon flour
1 teaspoon vinegar
600 ml / 1 pint water
salt
30 g / 1 oz diced onion
30 g / 1 oz butter
30 ml / 1 fl oz wine
24 mussels
300 ml / ½ pint double cream
1 sachet saffron
1 teaspoon *vinaigre de vin vieux*
6 vol-au-vent cases

Peel the salsify and cut into 1 cm / ½ inch lengths. Whisk the flour and vinegar into the pan of water. Add salt and bring to the boil. Simmer salsify in this liquid until tender, about 20 minutes. Drain the salsify but reserve a quarter of the liquid.

Sweat the onion in butter, add the wine and then mussels and cook until the mussels open. Shell them and reserve. Strain the liquor through a sieve and reserve it.

Put both reserved liquids in a pan and reduce to a glaze. Add cream and saffron and reduce to a coating consistency. Beat in the old wine vinegar. Add mussels and salsify to the pan and let them heat through. Spoon into six freshly baked vol-au-vent. If you mean to use up all the sauce, pour it so that it runs over the sides of the pastry and on to the plate (heresy!).

Turbot and Pine Kernel Turnovers

Serves 6
350 g / 12 oz puff pastry
1 tablespoon butter
50 g / 2 oz diced onion
1 pinch freshly ground coriander
   seeds
1 pinch freshly ground cumin
1 tablespoon pine kernels
150 g / 5 oz turbot fillet
150 g / 5 oz cooked potato
½ lime
salt
Tabasco
80 g / 3 oz strained Greek
   yoghourt
1 egg, beaten

Roll out the pastry and cut out six 12 cm / 5 inch circles. Melt the butter in a pan and fry the onion. When it starts to soften add the coriander and cumin. Add the pine kernels and turn up the heat. As they start to colour add diced turbot and potato. Squeeze the juice of the lime over the ingredients in the pan. Off the heat add salt, Tabasco and yoghourt. Cool the mixture.

Brush the pastry edges with beaten egg. Put neat piles of filling in the centre of each pastry circle. Bring the edges together and seal the pastry. Make a small cut in the tops, then brush them with beaten egg and bake 15 minutes in a hot oven, 220°C, 425°F, gas mark 7.

Cod Pasties

300 g / 10 oz flour
salt, pepper
150 g / 5 oz margarine
milk
175 g / 6 oz cod fillet
50 g / 2 oz butter
50 g / 2 oz diced onion
1 small grated carrot
50 g / 2 oz diced green streaky
   bacon, rind removed
115 g / 4 oz diced potato
50 g / 2 oz smoked cod's roe
1 tablespoon tomato ketchup
1 egg

Sift the flour with a pinch of salt. Rub the margarine into the flour and add enough milk to make a smooth dough. Work into a ball and divide into four. Roll out the pastry and cut out four 18 cm / 7 inch circles.

Chop the cod coarsely. Heat the butter in a pan and sweat the onion, carrot, bacon and potato in it. Once the potato has cooked through, stir in the cod off the heat together with cod's roe and ketchup. Check the seasoning.

Spoon the filling on to the four circles of pastry. Brush the edges with water and crimp the pasties. Make a small slit in the top of each one. Egg-wash the tops. Bake 35 minutes in a moderately hot oven, 190°C, 375°F, gas mark 5.

Monkfish Tourte

Serves 6–8
50 ml / 2 fl oz olive oil
1 onion, diced

Heat the olive oil and fry the onion in it. When it turns transparent add the capsicum. Fry 2 minutes then add the aubergine; it will guzzle up the oil and then sweat it

½ green capsicum, chopped
½ aubergine, cubed
2 cloves garlic, crushed
2 small courgettes, sliced
3 tomatoes, chopped
12 basil leaves
salt, pepper
450 g / 1 lb monkfish
butter
450 g / 1 lb rich shortcrust
   pastry (page 100)
1 tablespoon semolina
1 egg, beaten

out again as soon as it is cooked. When this happens add the garlic and courgettes. As soon as they start to soften add the tomatoes, basil, salt and pepper. Stir and cool.

Cut the fish into small cubes. Butter a 25 cm / 10 inch flan ring. Line it with two-thirds of the pastry and sprinkle semolina over the base. Fill with the vegetables and monkfish. Roll out the remaining pastry to make a pastry lid. Seal the edges. Glaze with egg. Make a hole for the steam to escape. Bake 35 minutes at 190°C, 375°F, gas mark 5. Turn out of the ring and serve hot.

Prawn and Mushroom Splits

Serves 6
450 g / 1 lb rich shortcrust (page
   100)
30 g / 1 oz butter
50 g / 2 oz mushrooms, finely
   sliced
1 clove garlic
sea salt, pepper
1 teaspoon lemon juice
80 g / 3 oz haricots verts
1 tomato
80 g / 3 oz shelled prawns
1 egg, beaten

Roll out the pastry and cut out six 12 cm / 5 inch circles. Heat the butter and fry the mushrooms. When they start to brown, add the garlic, crushed with sea salt and lemon juice. Take off the heat.

Cook the beans 3 minutes (longer if they are thick) in salted water and drain. Chop coarsely. Cut the tomato in 6 slices. Combine beans with mushrooms and add the prawns. Adjust the seasoning. Spoon on to the pastry circles and lay a tomato slice on top. Brush the edges with egg, bring them together and seal so that the joining rims stand upright. Brush with beaten egg, lay on a baking sheet and bake 20–25 minutes in a moderately hot oven, 190°C, 375°F, gas mark 5.

Smoked Salmon and Cream Cheese Tartlets

butter
350 g / 12 oz rich shortcrust
   pastry
1 teaspoon Dijon mustard
1 teaspoon lemon juice
1 egg + 1 yolk
150 ml / ¼ pint double cream
4 slices smoked salmon
80 g / 3 oz cream cheese

Butter four tartlet tins (11 cm / 4½ inches in diameter). Roll out the pastry as finely as you can. Cut out four pieces and line the tins. Rest 30 minutes. Line with baking parchment and fill the parchment with baking beans. Bake 15 minutes in a moderate oven, 180°C, 350°F, gas mark 4. Remove the beans and parchment.

Whisk mustard, lemon juice, egg, yolk and cream together. Put a generous slice of smoked salmon in the bottom of each tartlet. Dab walnut-sized pieces of cream cheese on the salmon. Pour over the custard mixture and bake 15–20 minutes at 230°C, 450°F, gas mark 8. Serve piping hot, perhaps with a cucumber and dill salad.

Rich Shortcrust Pastry

Rub 400 g / 14 oz good salted butter into 700 g / 1½ lb flour. Beat 4 eggs together and work them into the flour and fat so that the paste forms a smooth, almost silky, ball. A beater on a mixing machine or a food processor is as good as, if not better than, fingers.

Turbot Pie

50 g / 2 oz diced shallots
15 g / ½ oz diced celery
40 g / 1½ oz butter
150 ml / ¼ pint fish stock
3 sorrel leaves
175 ml / 6 fl oz double cream
salt, pepper
25 g / ¾ oz flour
1 teaspoon cider mustard
200 ml / 7 fl oz milk
40 g / 1½ oz mature Cheddar, grated
2 eggs + 1 white
175 g / 6 oz puff pastry (page 95)
4 × 80 g / 3 oz turbot fillets
4 scallops

Sweat the shallots (bar a tablespoon) and the celery in 30 g / 1 oz butter. Add the stock and sorrel and reduce to a glaze. Pour in the cream and boil the sauce back to a light coating consistency. Season.

Sweat the rest of the shallots in the remaining butter. Stir in the flour and mustard. Blend in the heated milk to form a thick sauce. Whisk in the cheese. Beat in 2 yolks. Whisk the 3 whites until stiff, fold into the soufflé base.

Roll out the pastry and cut into 1 cm / ½ inch strips. Lay them round the rims of four individual pie dishes. Poach the turbot fillets in salted water for 1 minute. Drain on absorbent paper.

Spoon 2 tablespoons of sauce in the bottom of each dish. Cover with turbot. Slice each scallop into 3 and lay it on the turbot. Spoon enough soufflé mixture on the fish to reach the pie dish rim. Bake 9 minutes at 230°C, 450°F, gas mark 8.

Done right, the pastry and soufflé rise and cook through, the turbot finishes cooking. The scallops heat through without toughening and the sauce is hot.

Fisherman's Jacket

4 large King Edward potatoes
oil
700 g / 1½ lb ling fillets
1 tablespoon cream

Scrub the potatoes, dry them and rub with oil. Bake in a hot oven until crisp. Slice off the tops and scoop out a bit more than half of the insides. Steam the ling over a pan of simmering water and let it drain for a few

2 teaspoons anchovy essence
300 ml / ½ pint béchamel sauce
40 g / 1½ oz grated Cheddar
salt, pepper

For the béchamel:
50 g / 2 oz butter
45 g / 1¾ oz flour
600 ml / 1 pint milk
1 small bayleaf
1 small onion
½ clove
salt, pepper

minutes. Stir cream and anchovy essence into the béchamel. Season. Divide the fish into four and put a piece in each potato. Pour over sauce, cover with grated cheese and glaze under a grill for 3 minutes.

Basic Béchamel

Melt the butter in an enamel, copper or stainless steel pan. Add the flour and work it with the butter into a sandy roux. Cook gently for a minute or so. Heat the milk and add it to the roux in three stages. Beat the sauce well after each addition. Pin the bayleaf to the onion with the clove and add it to the sauce. Season lightly and simmer for 1 hour, stirring from time to time to prevent the sauce from sticking.

Scallop and Aubergine Samosas

160 g / 5½ oz strained Greek
   yoghourt
220 g / 8 oz flour
2 tablespoons water
1 chilli, diced
7.5 cm / 3 inch piece of fresh
   ginger, finely diced
2 cloves garlic, crushed
80 g / 3 oz diced onion
50 g / 2 oz butter
175 g / 6 oz diced aubergine
3 scallops, diced
1 diced tomato
1 lime
salt, pepper
oil for frying

Mix 115 g / 4 oz yoghourt into the flour, add the water and work into a ball. Divide into three and roll into sausages. Cut each sausage in six. Roll out each piece very finely, cut into a 15 cm / 6 inch circle and halve it.

Combine chilli with a few seeds, ginger and garlic. Fry the onion in butter, add the chilli mixture and fry 1 more minute. Add aubergine and stew over a low flame until tender. Cool. Stir in the scallops, tomato, lime juice and the remaining yoghourt. Season.

Now comes the fiddly bit! Brush each pastry half-moon's edges with water. Form a conical pouch and press the seam going down to the cone point. Fill each pouch with the scallop and aubergine mixture. Press the curved edges together to seal in the filling. Deep fry the samosas in hot oil until golden, turning them in the oil after 2 minutes. Drain on absorbent paper, sprinkle with salt and serve while still hot and crisp.

Crab Tart with Wholemeal and Sesame Pastry

200 g / 7 oz wholemeal flour for baking
50 g / 2 oz butter
50 g / 2 oz lard
salt
1 tablespoon sesame seeds
3 tablespoons cold water
sesame oil
2 eggs + 1 yolk
250 ml / 9 fl oz cream
pepper
350 g / 12 oz crabmeat

Crumb the flour with the butter and lard. Mix in salt and sesame seeds. Add the cold water and work into a ball. Rest 30 minutes, roll out on a floured surface, and line a 20 cm / 8 inch tart ring which has been brushed with sesame oil. Let the pastry rest again. Cover the uncooked pastry with oiled greaseproof paper and fill it with baking beans. Bake 20 minutes at 190°C, 375°F, gas mark 5. Whisk the eggs and cream and season. Sprinkle the crabmeat over the base of the tart, pour over the egg and cream. Bake for about 25 minutes, until set.

Seafood Pancakes

50 g / 2 oz flour + 1 extra tablespoon
salt, pepper
1 egg + 1 yolk
115 ml / 4 fl oz milk
lard
8 button onions, peeled
50 g / 2 oz butter
1 tablespoon dry white wine
4 scallops
175 g / 6 oz monkfish
1 teaspoon chopped parsley
1 teaspoon chopped chervil
2 tablespoons double cream
¼ lemon
115 g / 4 oz mushrooms

Sift the flour with a pinch of salt. Make a batter with flour, one egg and milk. Leave to stand 1 hour. Brush a large pancake pan with lard and fry 4 pancakes.

Put the button onions in a pan with half the butter and a tablespoon of water. Cover and stew very slowly 45 minutes. (This can be done while the batter is resting.) Reserve.

Boil 300 ml / ½ pint of water with the white wine. Add the scallops and monkfish cut in 1 cm / ½ inch cubes. Simmer 3 minutes and drain the fish; reserve the liquid.

Make a roux with the remaining butter and the tablespoon of flour. Add the reserved liquid. Simmer 15 minutes. Stir in parsley and chervil.

Whisk together the egg yolk, cream and a small squeeze of lemon. When this liaison starts to thicken beat it into the hot white sauce and adjust the seasoning. Slice the mushrooms and add them to the sauce along with the onions, monkfish and scallops. Fill the pancakes with this mixture, roll them up, cover with more sauce and put under the grill for 2 minutes at most.

Poor Man's Fish

*Supper, in fact, is the meal of many inventions, including all sorts of crabs,
little lobsters and such unsaleable fish as duncow (dog-fish), conger, skate or
weever, together with dree-hap'orth, or a pint, of stout and bitter from the
Alexandra.*

Stephen Reynolds, *A Poor Man's House*

Beer hardly merits the title of fishing village today. A few broad-beamed
boats rest upon the steep shingle when they are not out in the bay servicing
crab pots or, in summer, plying anglers and trippers. Once it was a working,
though hardly prosperous haven, rather than the sleepy suburb of the sleepy
seaside town of Seaton.

Jack Rattenbury, the smuggler, grew up in the village. His mother hawked
fish. He started going to sea with his uncle at the age of nine, but ended his
apprenticeship abruptly when he was beaten with a rope-end for losing a rudder
in Lyme harbour. Throughout the Napoleonic wars he covered his smuggling
activities by posing as a fisherman. His autobiography shows that he earned far
more respect and status from his clandestine profession than his legitimate one.
Even then, fishermen would encourage their sons to work on the land instead of
going to sea.

The last fishing family in Beer are the Newtons. The father minds the shop
which abuts the beach; sons and one grandson take out a 35 foot trawler, the

Arandora Star. Most of the holidaymakers who call at Beer Fisheries demand fillets of plaice or prawns, the one bought from Plymouth and the other out of the deep-freeze. They turn up their noses at the conger, the skate, the huss, the pollack, the pout whiting, the dabs, the flounder and the gurnards. A generation ago, these fish were so plentiful that 'Captain' Newton remembers them being used by gardeners as fertilizers. Now the supply just about matches the demand.

Of all the lesser-known species, dog-fish are the most prolific. A relative of the shark, they grow to two or three feet long. Their skin is speckled and rough like sandpaper. On board trawlers, fishermen will always clean and skin them as quickly as possible, because the skin peels off readily when they are fresh. In the shop, you can tell whether the fish is newly in. The ribbed muscles are still red, whereas they will turn brown within a day. 'Dogs' have a single cartilaginous backbone which makes them easy eating; their flesh is firm when just cooked, but turns dry and woolly when left too long in the pan or pot.

Conger eel has a reputation for feeding on the corpses of drowned men, but it only takes the freshest bait. Fishermen who trap them in set nets often discover that they have spent their time, like the proverbial condemned man, dining off the plumpest among the other fish. Were it not for the lethal bones, particularly those at the tail end, eels would be among the most sought-after seafood delicacies. A conger head costs nothing but will make some of the best fish soup. Soupe d'Andgulle is a speciality of Jersey, combining conger and cabbage, flavoured with borage leaves and coloured with marigold petals. The flesh is so firm, gelatinous and meaty that it can take up to an hour to cook.

Stubby, large-eyed pout whiting have a lovely silvery bloom when they emerge from the sea. It soon disappears, leaving the dead fish flaccid and uninteresting. Crimped, floured and fried while still at its best, pout whiting is an entirely different proposition, sweet, juicy and delicately flavoured.

Another undervalued fish is the gurnard or gurnet. There are many varieties ranging in colour from fawn to bright carrot. Their knobbly heads and tapering bodies do not look promising. The spiny dorsal fins can easily spike unwary hands; they are the first thing to remove when boning the fish. Once that has been dealt with gurnards can be cooked whole or filleted as you will. Because the French refer to the red gurnard as *rouget-grondin*, it is often compared unfavourably with red mullet (French: *rouget*), which is unfair. Mullets taste best grilled or fried, but gurnards are more a fish for soups and stews.

Among flat fish, flukes (flounder) and megrim are hardly worth the effort of cooking. In a fish hierarchy, if such a thing existed, they rank below plaice in both taste and texture. The dab, on the other hand, scores higher marks. It looks a bit like a plaice, minus the orange spots, and is both smaller and narrower. The skin is roughish and needs scraping before cooking.

Few inshore fishermen go out in winter. The largest trawler at Lyme shies from a force seven wind. That means locally caught herring are scarce even in December, the high season. For two or three days at a time during that month, the prevailing westerlies will drop, the sea settle to a treacle-smooth calm and the odd boat will set sail. The slate-blue herring which it brings back are plump and rich. You can eat the fillets raw with salt and onion as the Dutch do: *Hollandse nieuwe* are even better than *matjes*, the sweet-pickled herring sold in delicatessens. A fat herring, one rich in oil, will weigh 30 per cent more than a lean one of the same length.

Dab in Cream

Serves 1
1 × 350 g / 12 oz dab
30 g / 1 oz butter
1 clove
1 mint leaf
150 ml / ¼ pint double cream
salt, pepper

Scale the dab, rinse it and pat dry. Clip off the fins. Butter an oval ovenproof dish of similar size to the dab. Flick the knobbly end off a clove and put it in the dish together with the mint. Lay the dab on top and pour over the cream. Season and bake in a moderate oven, 180°C, 350°F, gas mark 4, until the cream has boiled and thickened. This takes about 20 minutes.

Dab and Walnut Fricassée

Serves 2
50 g / 2 oz shelled walnuts
5 tablespoons sunflower oil
1 tablespoon dry white wine
150 ml / ¼ pint fish stock
1 level teaspoon caster sugar
salt
1 dessertspoon rich soy sauce
1 heaped teaspoon arrowroot
2 large dabs, filleted
115 g / 4 oz grated carrots
115 g / 4 oz mushrooms, sliced
4 shallots, diced
1 clove garlic, crushed
1 tablespoon walnut oil

Soak the walnuts in water for 1 hour, drop them into boiling water 2 minutes. Drain and rub off as much skin as will come away easily. Heat 3 tablespoons of oil in a pan. Fry the nuts slowly until they start to brown and become crunchy. Drain them on absorbent paper.

Mix the wine, stock, sugar, salt, soy sauce and arrowroot in a jug.

Skin the dab fillets and cut them into strips.

Heat 2 tablespoons of oil in a pan. Sauté the carrots, mushrooms and shallots for a minute, add the dabs and sauté a minute more. Stir the liquid in the jug, pour it over the fish and vegetables and heat until thickened. Add the garlic and check the seasoning. Add the walnuts to the sauce and the walnut oil.

Serve with noodles.

Duncow Casserole

4 baby turnips
salt, freshly ground black pepper
12 small new potatoes
50 g / 2 oz carrot
50 g / 2 oz celeriac
50 g / 2 oz parsnip
700 g / 1½ lb huss
flour
50 ml / 2 fl oz clarified butter
150 g / 5 oz diced onion
1 teaspoon chopped rosemary
2 teaspoons tomato purée
200 ml / 7 fl oz dry white wine
2 teaspoons chopped parsley

Peel and quarter the turnips and boil in lightly salted water. Drain and reserve the cooking liquid. Boil the new potatoes. Cut the carrot, celeriac and parsnip into matchsticks. Cut the huss into 2.5 cm / 1 inch thick steaks. Dust with flour and fry in clarified butter.

Add the onion to the pan, together with rosemary and tomato purée. Cook 2 minutes. Pour over the wine and 400 ml / ⅔ pint of turnip stock. Boil and add the matchsticks of vegetables. After 2 minutes, drain the fish and vegetables with a slotted spoon. Reduce the liquid by half. Add the turnips and potatoes, and when they have heated through add the fish, matchsticks of vegetables, parsley and plenty of black pepper.

Duncow in Sour Sauce

700 g / 1½ lb huss
1 tablespoon dry white wine
115 ml / 4 fl oz sesame oil
220 g / 8 oz tomatoes
3 tubers krachai (see below)
1 heaped teaspoon caster sugar
1 heaped teaspoon soft brown
    sugar
150 ml / ¼ pint water
5 tablespoons vinegar
50 g / 2 oz mushrooms, chopped
1 heaped teaspoon tomato purée
3 tablespoons red capsicum cut
    into thin strips
salt
1 teaspoon arrowroot
3 tablespoons lean ham cut into
    thin strips,
3 tablespoons spring onion cut
    lengthwise into thin strips

Bone the huss. Cut it into pieces roughly 5 cm / 2 inches long. Marinate half an hour in the wine and a teaspoon of sesame oil.

Skin, seed and chop the tomatoes. Finely dice the krachai. Put the sugar in a pan with the water. Bring to the boil, stirring to dissolve it. Add the vinegar, mushrooms, tomato purée, tomatoes, capsicum, krachai and a little salt. Simmer 10 minutes. Dissolve the arrowroot in 2 tablespoons of water. Whisk into the sauce. Boil and add the ham and spring onion.

Heat the rest of the oil. Fry the fish for 3 minutes. Drain on absorbent paper, transfer to a serving dish and pour over the sauce.

NOTE: krachai is a member of the ginger family and has bunches of thin tubers with a mild ginger flavour. It is imported from Thailand where it is commonly used as a seasoning.

Fried Dabs with Hot Capsicum Relish

2 capsicums (or 4 half capsicums
   of different hues)
2 dried chillies
80 ml / 3 fl oz sunflower oil for
   frying
salt, pepper
juice of 1 orange
1 tablespoon olive oil
4 dabs
flour

Slice the seeded capsicums and dice the chillies. Heat a tablespoon of sunflower oil in a non-stick pan, add the capsicums, chillies including any seeds and a little salt. Cover and stew over a low flame for 10–15 minutes. Remove the lid and turn up the heat until the capsicum skins start to char. Turn them into a clean bowl and pour over orange juice and olive oil.

Fillet and skin the dabs and dust with seasoned flour. Fry them in hot oil for 2–3 minutes. Arrange the fish on a plate surrounded with capsicums and marinade.

Fried Whiting with Savoy Cabbage and Kidney Beans

1 medium Savoy cabbage
salt, pepper
175 g / 6 oz cooked red kidney
   beans
1 onion, diced
30 g / 1 oz butter + 60 ml /
   2 fl oz clarified butter
1 clove garlic
1 teaspoon Tabasco
80 g / 3 oz Cheddar, grated
4 × 350 g / 12 oz whiting
flour

Shred the cabbage and boil in salted water for a few minutes until just cooked. Drain and combine with kidney beans.

Fry the onion in 30 g / 1 oz butter until golden. Add garlic, Tabasco and cheese.

Cut the heads and tails off the whiting. Dust them with seasoned flour and fry in the clarified butter for 4 minutes on either side. Drain on absorbent paper and serve on a bed of cabbage and beans.

Herring Baked with Tomato and Spinach

4 herrings
salt, pepper
1 beef tomato
1 onion, finely sliced
30 g / 1 oz butter
450 g / 1 lb spinach

Fillet the herrings and lay them in a buttered ovenproof dish. Season. Slice the tomato and lay it over the fish. Arrange the onion slices on top. Season and brush with melted butter. Blanch the spinach and press out excess moisture. Spread the leaves over the tomato and onion. Cover with buttered foil and bake 45 minutes in a low oven, 160°C, 325°F, gas mark 3.

Gratin of Plaice with Butter Bean Stew

220 g / 8 oz butter beans
salt, pepper
160 g / 5½ oz butter
4 teaspoons chopped rosemary
2 teaspoons chopped mint
1 teaspoon chopped fennel leaves
1 pinch dried thyme
4 finely diced shallots
4 chopped tomatoes
4 plaice fillets
80 g / 3 oz wholemeal
    breadcrumbs

Cook the butter beans in salted water. The time varies according to freshness, but should be around the hour mark.

Melt 115 g / 4 oz butter in a pan, add the rosemary, mint, fennel and thyme. Add the shallots and sweat over a low heat, then add the tomatoes. Stew 3–4 minutes and combine with the butter beans. Season.

Put a layer of beans on four individual gratin dishes. Lay a plaice fillet on top. Put a little butter on the plaice and cover with a layer of breadcrumbs. Cook in a very hot oven, 230°C, 450°F, gas mark 8 until the crumbs form a golden crust.

Ling in Dark Brown Rum

300 ml / ½ pint boiling water
30 g / 1 oz sultanas
50 g / 2 oz butter
1 heaped teaspoon soft brown
    sugar
4 × 150 g / 5 oz ling fillets
1 lime
4 tablespoons dark rum

Pour the boiling water over the sultanas and steep for 15 minutes before draining them. Heat the butter with the sugar. Brush a sheet of foil with half the mixture. Lay the 4 fillets on top and coat with the remaining sugar and butter. Thinly slice the lime and put the rings on the fish. Spoon over the sultanas and the rum, seal the foil packages and bake 20 minutes in a moderate oven, 190°C, 375°F, gas mark 5.

Plaice Fillets in Milk with Mashed Sweet Potato

450 g / 1 lb sweet potato
50 g / 2 oz butter
150 ml / ¼ pint milk
salt
4 large plaice fillets
1 tomato
1 tablespoon chopped parsley

Peel and chop the sweet potato, boil it and mash by hand, adding 40 g / 1½ oz butter. Brush a pan with the remaining butter. Add milk and a pinch of salt. Bring to simmering point. Put the plaice fillets in the milk and cook 4 minutes, basting them frequently. Lay the fillets on a bed of sweet potato. Chop the skinned and seeded tomato and add it to the milk with chopped parsley. Spoon some of the mixture over the fish.

Monkfish and Kidney Bean Stew

80 g / 3 oz kidney beans (soaked
  overnight)
salt, pepper
220 g / 8 oz diced onion
50 g / 2 oz butter
1 teaspoon molasses sugar
2 cloves garlic, crushed
1 teaspoon Mexican chilli powder
1 pinch ground coriander
450 g / 1 lb tomatoes
800 g / 1¾ lb monkfish
1 teaspoon chopped parsley
1 teaspoon chopped fresh
  coriander

Put the beans in a pan of cold water, boil 10 minutes
and drain. Put them in a fresh pan of salted water and
simmer until tender.

Sweat the onion in butter until soft, add the sugar,
garlic, chilli and coriander. Cook for 2 minutes. Drop
the tomatoes in boiling water for 12 seconds, drain,
skin, seed and chop the flesh. Add them to the onion
mixture. Stew 15 minutes over a low heat and season
heavily. Stir the beans into the sauce.

Chop the monkfish in strips, lay them on the bean
stew and steam until just cooked. Sprinkle parsley and
coriander leaves over the fish.

NOTE: monkfish, alas, is no longer a 'poor man's fish'. As recently
as the mid-70s you could buy it, ready skinned, for less than 40p
per pound.

Huss and Green Lentils

150 g / 5 oz green lentils
1 clove
1 bayleaf
1 onion
1 carrot
salt, pepper
1 tablespoon English mustard
80 g / 3 oz diced shallots
2 tablespoons cider vinegar
6 tablespoons sunflower oil
1 teaspoon garam masala
2 tablespoons flour
450 g / 1 lb huss
80 g / 3 oz clarified butter
1 heaped tablespoon chopped
  parsley
2 chopped tomatoes

Boil the lentils with the clove, bayleaf, onion, carrot
and salt until cooked (about 30 minutes). Drain. Blend
the mustard, shallots, vinegar, oil, salt and pepper into
a vinaigrette. Mix it with the lentils.

Mix the garam masala and flour together. Chop the
huss into lozenges 2.5 cm / 1 inch thick and coat them
in spiced flour. Melt the butter in a pan and fry the huss
over a high flame, turning the pieces often. Add parsley
and tomatoes to the pan and shake well.

Spoon the still warm lentils into bowls and arrange
the fish on top.

Spicy Sprats with Mint Sauce

700 g / 1 ½ lb sprats
milk
salt
flour
clarified butter or oil

For the spice mixture:
1 teaspoon each coriander seeds,
    cumin, black peppercorns
½ teaspoon mustard seeds
½ teaspoon turmeric
½ teaspoon grated dry ginger
    root
4 hulled cardamom pods
3 heaped tablespoons flour
salt

For the sauce:
115 g / 4 oz strained Greek
    yoghourt
115 g / 4 oz fromage blanc
½ clove garlic
salt
1 tablespoon grated onion
1 teaspoon chopped mint
lemon juice

You can still buy a bucket of sprats for £1 when they are abundant. Stay within sniffing distance of the pan when you fry them, so that you can eat them with your fingers while they are still piping hot. To do this, hold the sprat by the head, bite off the tail which is crisp, then nibble your way up either side of the backbone.

Rinse and drain the sprats. Put them in a pan or dish with milk to cover, then dip them in seasoned flour and fry, a few at a time, in hot clarified butter or oil for 3 minutes on either side. Season.

   Alternatively, you can try this spice mixture. Roast the coriander, cumin, peppercorns and mustard in a dry pan over a low flame for 4 minutes, shaking the pan. Blend these spices with the other ingredients in a spice mill and mix them with the flour before coating the sprats.

Mint Sauce
Combine the yoghourt and fromage blanc. Crush the garlic with salt, and add to the sauce with the onion and mint. Stir in lemon juice to taste. Leave in the fridge for a few hours to amalgamate the flavours.

Whiting and Gratinated Chicory

65 g / 2 ½ oz butter
1 tablespoon soft brown sugar
1 lemon
4 heads chicory
salt, pepper
4 × 150 g / 5 oz whiting fillets
50 g / 2 oz breadcrumbs

Butter an ovenproof dish. Heat the rest of the butter with sugar and lemon juice in a pan until the sugar dissolves. Split the bases of the chicory and lay them in the dish. Pour the butter, lemon and sugar over them. Season, cover and bake 40 minutes in a hottish oven, 200°C, 400°F, gas mark 6, basting once or twice. Take the dish from the oven and turn up the heat to 220°C, 425°F, gas mark 7. Hide a whiting fillet under each head of chicory. Sprinkle breadcrumbs on top and moisten with pan juices. Return to the oven uncovered for 10 minutes until the breadcrumbs start to brown, and serve.

Overboard and Over the Top

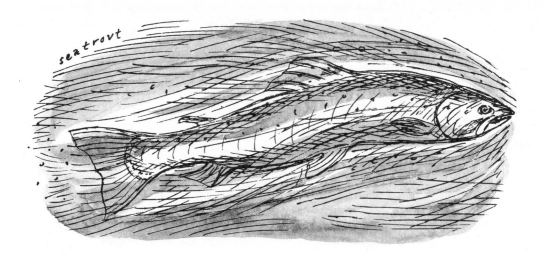

seatrout

*The essence of your cooking is not the shedding of blood, sweat and tears to
impress people at any cost, but the thoughtful pleasure you obtain from doing
simple things skilfully, efficiently and imaginatively.*

Le Menu Gastronomique by Jack Gillon

Baked red snapper . . . with confit of vegetables . . . fried onion rings . . .
pepper tartlets . . . and two pepper sauces. When the host, hostess, cook or
chef goes to such elaborate lengths to mix so many textures and flavours on a
single plate, you cannot help wondering whether he or she is trying harder to
impress than to please.

It is very true that some of the world's finest cooks are exhibitionists, but
because they are securely confident of their ability, they are careful to exhibit
just so much of their skill without going wildly over the top. They never lose
contact with their audience. By contrast, if you let a narcissist loose in the
kitchen, even a technically clever one, it is odds on that he will always put a
cherry too many on his fairy cakes.

The vices of modern foodies are more discreet than those of the Mrs Beeton
era. Then the approach to middle-class food was unashamedly ostentatious, an
equivalent of Victorian Gothic on the plate. Sculptured details took precedence
over edible ones. Our excesses are more palatable, more discreet, though in
some ways they are more affected than ever before.

It's not the carving of rose petals out of tomato peel which is to blame, nor the turning of carrots into barrels and lozenges. They are merely a part of the classical baggage which has been adopted by a handful of chic hostelries. What jars more is the expertly positioned radicchio leaf, the three mangetouts forming a neat fan and the pair of spring carrots pointing like fingers at a distant cube of steak on the far side of the plate. These would-be aesthetic gestures shift the balance from eating as a pleasurable experience, fulfilling a basic animal need, to a pseudo-artistic plane where feeding is incidental and appetite has no place.

It may well be that efforts of this kind are inspired by European contact with Japan, but an occidental misses the point if he think he can ape Japanese subtlety by putting less on a plate. One modern haiku (a 17-syllable poem) mocks the barbarism of our cherished eating habits:

> In Occidental culinary art
> Every bleeding plate is round.

A Japanese meal at its most sophisticated is no more about the food than a tea ceremony is about tea. Interwoven in the event are strands of religion, philosophy, art, tradition and technique.

What nouvelle cuisine can claim as its contribution to Western cookery is a mixture of curiosity and inventiveness rather than artistic or aesthetic value. Cooking is a Game you can Eat (the title of a children's book) would make a fine motto for the innovators of the modern generation, if they did not take themselves so seriously. There is literally no limit to the combinations of ingredients or to the variety of recipes which can be concocted. The trick is in the blending and in knowing when to stop. Paul Bocuse, the high priest of modern cookery, turned apostate from the school which he, more than any of his peers, is responsible for founding, when a colleague served him a Chanel No 5 sorbet. Enough was enough.

Unless he can afford to buy Dover sole every day, it is a brave person who will risk dousing it in a raspberry vinegar and green peppercorn sauce, when he can pop it under the grill with a knob of butter, leave it five minutes and know that it will taste wonderful. But applying one's imagination to food-play is addictive. It is hard to resist simple, comestible syllogisms of the kind: 'A tastes good with B; B tastes good with C, so why not try cooking A, B and C together?' Unfortunately the success rating of such experiments is low. Each time you add an extra ingredient to this hypothetical witches' cauldron, the murkier the brew is likely to turn. And yet, and yet, cooks persist; and still, every so often, a new combination emerges which, heaven alone knows why, works. The question is: for whom, or alternatively, for how long? The taste which suits one generation may repel another.

'Suppose,' wrote the Dutch philosopher Erasmus, 'a man were eating stock-fish, the smell of which would choke another, and yet believed it a dish for the Gods, what difference is there to his happiness?'

Baked Hake with Pickled Onions and Sultanas

4 × 200 g / 7 oz hake steaks
salt, pepper
15 g / ½ oz butter
150 ml / ¼ pint water
50 ml / 2 fl oz wine vinegar
1 tablespoon white wine
4 tomatoes
12 pickling onions, peeled
4 coriander seeds
parsley stalks, thyme, 1 bayleaf
1 tablespoon soft brown sugar
30 g / 1 oz sultanas
1 tablespoon olive oil

Season the hake and wrap each one in a sheet of buttered foil. Bring the water to the boil, add vinegar and wine. Skin and seed the tomatoes and add them and onions to the pan of water, wine and vinegar. Season with coriander, herbs, sugar and salt. Throw in the sultanas. Simmer 90 minutes without boiling. Take out the onions. Reduce the liquid till it is thick. Stir in the oil. Bake the hake 20 minutes at 200°C, 400°F, gas mark 6. Unwrap and dish up with onion and sultana sauce.

This is also good cold.

Baked Seatrout Steaks, Red and Green Cabbage

450 g / 1 lb red cabbage
salt, pepper
80 g / 3 oz butter
1 teaspoon molasses sugar
1 tablespoon cider vinegar
2 tablespoons grated apple
  (Cox's)
450 g / 1 lb green cabbage
1 teaspoon caraway seeds
1 pinch ground coriander
4 × 175 g / 6 oz seatrout steaks

Shred the red cabbage with a stainless steel knife. Cook in salted water and drain. Heat 15 g / ½ oz butter in a pan and add the molasses sugar. Stir until the sugar is dissolved and add the red cabbage. Pour over the cider vinegar and turn up the heat. Coat the red cabbage in butter, vinegar and sugar. Take off the heat and stir in the apple.

Shred the green cabbage and boil in salted water for a few minutes till tender. Drain thoroughly. Heat 15 g / ½ ounce of butter in a pan, add the spices, cook slowly for 2 minutes without letting the butter burn, then stir in the cabbage.

Season the seatrout and wrap in buttered foil. Bake 20 minutes at 200°C, 400°F, gas mark 6.

For each portion, cover half a dinner plate with red and half with green cabbage. Take the seatrout out of the foil and lay in the middle of each plate.

Fillets of Lemon Sole with Avocado Sauce

1 small avocado
50 ml / 2 fl oz chicken stock
1 shallot, diced
1 teaspoon lemon juice
115 ml / 4 fl oz double cream
1 gherkin, diced
1 heaped teaspoon chopped
    fennel leaves
50 ml / 2 fl oz low fat yoghourt
salt, cayenne pepper
4 filleted lemon soles

Liquidize the avocado with the chicken stock, shallot, lemon juice and cream. Simmer without boiling. Add the gherkin, fennel leaves, yoghourt and a pinch of cayenne pepper. Steam the lemon soles over a pan of water and season. Spoon the hot sauce on four dinner plates and arrange the fish on top.

Lemon Sole with Sweetcorn Fritters and Cream Sauce

175 g / 6 oz sweetcorn kernels
80 g / 3 oz flour
2 teaspoons baking powder
salt, pepper
2 small eggs
50 ml / 2 fl oz milk
30 g / 1 oz butter
30 ml / 1 fl oz oil
4 lemon soles, filleted
115 ml / 4 fl oz dry white wine
1 tablespoon diced shallot
1 tablespoon cognac
300 ml / ½ pint double cream
fresh chervil

Roughly chop the sweetcorn. Sift the flour and baking powder with a pinch of salt. Beat the eggs into the flour, then the corn, then the milk. Melt a little butter and oil in a frying pan. Fry the corn fritters, about a tablespoon of the mixture for each one. Turn them when they start to puff. Keep hot.

Put the fish in an ovenproof dish with white wine, shallot and seasoning. Cover with buttered foil. Bake 8 minutes in a hot oven, 220°C, 425°F, gas mark 7. Drain the fillets on absorbent paper. Reduce the liquid in the dish to a glaze. Add cognac and flame. Pour in the cream and reduce to a coating consistency. Adjust the seasoning. Arrange the fillets on four plates. Coat with sauce, garnish with chervil and serve with sweetcorn fritters.

Steamed Slip Soles with Orange and Green Peppercorns

4 × 150 g / 5 oz King Edward
    potatoes
4 navel oranges

Slip soles are small Dover soles which are sold for around half the price because of their size. They taste the same as any other Dover sole.

2 teaspoons green peppercorns +
  a few extra
sea salt
1 tablespoon chopped parsley
4 × 200 g / 7 oz slip soles
40 g / 1½ oz butter
80 g / 3 oz fresh goat's cheese
1 tablespoon chopped chives
pepper

Bake the potatoes for 1 hour in a hot oven, 200°C, 400°F, gas mark 6. Cut the tops and bottoms off the oranges. Stand them on a plate, slice away the peel and with it the outer membranes of the orange segments. Cut out the individual segments and reserve any juice on the plate.

Crush the peppercorns with a tablespoon of orange juice and a few grains of sea salt. Mix with chopped parsley.

Skin the soles and steam them over a pan of simmering water for 2–3 minutes. Scrape away the fins and arrange the soles on a dish. Brush with hot melted butter. Sprinkle the peppercorn and parsley mixture over them and add a few extra peppercorns. Garnish with orange segments. Keep hot.

Scoop out the insides of the potatoes and mix with the goat's cheese. Add pepper. Return the meal to the potatoes, garnish with chives and serve them as an accompaniment for the soles.

Lemon Sole with Juniper Sauce

1 heaped teaspoon finely chopped
  herbs (thyme, rosemary,
  savory)
8 black peppercorns, crushed
sea salt, pepper
6 juniper berries
4 lemon soles, filleted
30 g / 1 oz butter
3 tablespoons fish stock
1 tablespoon dry white vermouth
1 small bayleaf
150 ml / ¼ pint double cream

Combine the herbs with peppercorns, sea salt and 1 crushed juniper berry. Set aside. Put the lemon sole fillets in a buttered ovenproof dish. Season with salt and pepper, cover with buttered foil and bake 6 minutes in a hot oven, 220°C, 425°F, gas mark 7.

Reduce the stock and vermouth to a glaze with the bayleaf and 5 juniper berries, roughly crushed. Add any liquor rendered by the fish to the glaze. Whisk in the cream and reduce to a coating consistency. Season and strain the sauce on to four dinner plates. Arrange the fillets on top and sprinkle the savoury salt over them.

NOTE: juniper berries vary greatly in their intensity of flavour, so you may need more or less than the number given in this recipe.

John Dory on a Buckwheat Pancake with Bacon and Leek

½ teaspoon dried yeast
80 ml / 3 fl oz milk
30 g / 1 oz flour
15 g / ½ oz buckwheat flour
1 egg, separated
15 g / ½ oz melted butter
1 teaspoon dark brown sugar
salt, pepper
220 g / 8 oz leeks
2 John Dory (about 220 g / 8 oz
  each) filleted
30 g / 1 oz butter
300 ml / ½ pint béchamel sauce
  (page 101)
1 tablespoon cream
4 rashers green streaky bacon,
  rind removed

Dissolve the yeast in milk at blood temperature. Combine with a mixture of flour and buckwheat flour. Leave in a warm place until the 'sponge' doubles its volume. Separate the egg, beat the yolk with melted butter and brown sugar and mix into the flour and yeast. Let the dough rise again. Then whisk the egg white with a small pinch of salt and fold it into the risen dough. Brush a pan with butter and fry 4 buckwheat pancakes, roughly 10 cm / 4 inches in diameter, one by one. Keep hot.

Cook the leek, cut into rings, in salted water. Fry the John Dory in a little butter, or steam over seaweed. Heat the béchamel, season and stir in the cream.

Grill the bacon until very crisp. Put one pancake on a dinner plate, cover with leek. Arrange fish on top and coat with sauce. Lay a rasher of bacon on top. Repeat with the remaining pancakes.

Poached Skate Wings with Smoked Haddock Relish

30 g / 1 oz shallot
30 g / 1 oz carrot
15 g / ½ oz unsalted butter
300 ml / ½ pint milk
nutmeg
175 g / 6 oz smoked haddock
  fillet
4 × 175 g / 6 oz skate wings
1 tablespoon lemon juice or wine
  vinegar
sea salt
2 tablespoons double cream
3 spring onions (green parts only)
30 g / 1 oz clarified butter

Dice shallots and carrots as finely as possible. Melt the butter in a frying pan. Stew the carrots and shallots over a low heat. Add milk, nutmeg and smoked haddock. Poach the fish until it is cooked. Remove the fish, skin it and flake with a fork.

Put the skate in a pan with water, lemon juice or vinegar, and salt. Poach 10 minutes, drain, remove the white skin and keep the wings hot. Reduce the milk rapidly until most of it has evaporated then beat in the cream. Return the haddock to the pan with the tops of the spring onions cut into rings.

To serve, arrange the skate on preheated plates and brush with hot clarified butter. Sprinkle with a few grains of sea salt and surround with the flaked haddock and sauce.

Red Mullet St Amour

30 g / 1 oz smoked cod's roe
1 tablespoon double cream
¼ clove garlic
1 teaspoon lemon juice
4 teaspoons olive oil
4 red mullet fillets
175 g / 6 oz mild cure green
  streaky bacon, rind removed
2 rounded teaspoons soft brown
  sugar
150 ml / ¼ pint chicken stock
150 ml / ¼ pint St Amour
  (Beaujolais cru)
2 tablespoons chopped parsley
4 heart-shaped slices of bread
  fried in olive oil
sea salt, pepper

Liquidize the cod's roe with cream, garlic, lemon juice and 1 teaspoon olive oil. Brush a non-stick pan with the remaining olive oil. Fry the mullet about 2 minutes on each side. Keep hot. Dice the bacon and fry in the pan in which the mullet was cooked. As soon as it starts to colour add soft brown sugar and continue cooking until the bacon is coloured and glazed. Take the bacon from the pan and keep hot. Deglaze the pan with chicken stock and Beaujolais. Reduce to about 6 tablespoons of liquid. Return the fish and bacon to the pan and baste with the reduced sauce. Check the seasoning and sprinkle lavishly with parsley.

Spread some cod's roe pâté on the croûtons and arrange on a dish with mullet fillets, bacon and sauce.

NOTE: any Beaujolais may be substituted, although it would be a pity not to have the name.

Seatrout Gougère

115 g / 4 oz butter
175 ml / 6 fl oz water
80 g / 3 oz flour
50 g / 2 oz grated unpasteurized
  Cheddar
2 large eggs
700 g / 1½ lb seatrout
150 ml / ¼ pint dry cider
150 ml / ¼ pint fish stock
200 ml / 7 fl oz double cream
salt, pepper
1 teaspoon chopped coriander
  leaves + a few extra leaves

Put three-quarters of the butter in a pan with water and bring to a rolling boil. Beat in sifted flour and stir until the dough comes away from the sides of the pan. Off the heat beat in the cheese and then, one at a time, the eggs.

Fill a piping bag, fitted with a plain tube, with the mixture and pipe four rings on to a baking sheet. Bake 20–25 minutes in a hot oven, 220°C, 425°F, gas mark 7.

Cut the seatrout into pieces 5 cm / 2 inches long by 1 cm / ½ inch thick. Put in a pan with cider and fish stock. Bring to the boil and take out the fish. Reduce the liquid to a glaze and whisk in the cream. Reduce again, season and beat in the rest of the butter. Add the chopped coriander to the sauce.

Put the gougères on four dinner plates, fill the rings with seatrout, pour over the sauce and garnish with a few coriander leaves.

Spiced Chicken Turbot with Aubergines

2 teaspoons coriander seeds
1 teaspoon ground ginger
½ teaspoon cumin
1 teaspoon black peppercorns
1 pinch poppy seeds
sea salt
1 × 1.5 kg / 3½ lb turbot
1 lemon
1 aubergine
80 ml / 3 fl oz olive oil

Chicken turbot are young, small fish weighing under 4 lbs.

Pound the coriander, ginger, cumin, peppercorns, poppy seeds and a little salt in a mortar. Fillet and skin the turbot. Rub the spices on to the rounded side of each fillet and a little on the flat sides. Leave 1 hour.

Meanwhile top and tail the lemon, slice off the outer peel and cut the fruit into thin slices. Salt each slice and leave 1 hour. During this time slice and salt the aubergine. Let it drain in a colander for an hour, rinse and squeeze out excess moisture. Fry the aubergine in half the oil.

Heat the remaining oil in another pan and fry the turbot fillets for about 6 minutes. Put them on dinner plates, line a row of aubergine on top and garnish with the salted lemon slices.

Turbot Kedgeree

115 g / 4 oz diced onion
70 g / 2½ oz butter
115 g / 4 oz basmati rice
saffron or turmeric (optional)
salt
220 g / 8 oz Finnan haddock
150 ml / ¼ pint milk
4 × 80 g / 3 oz turbot fillets
1 tablespoon chopped fresh
    coriander

For the pickled mango:
3 tablespoons vinegar
250 g / 9 oz light soft brown
    sugar
½ stick cinnamon
1 pinch allspice
1 mango

Sweat the onion in 30 g / 1 oz butter, add the rice and fry for a couple of minutes. Add one and a half times the rice's volume of water, the saffron and a little salt. Cover and simmer 20 minutes.

Poach the haddock in milk for 2–3 minutes; discard skin and bones. Add the poaching liquid to the rice and boil hard, uncovered, until it has evaporated. Add flaked haddock.

Heat the remaining butter in a frying pan. Fry the turbot fillets for 3–4 minutes. Sprinkle with coriander, turn and cook for 15 seconds so that the coriander adheres to the fish. Serve the turbot on a bed of rice, garnished with pickled mango, cut into a fan-shape.

Pickled Mango (prepared in advance)
Put vinegar in a pan with water to make 300 ml / ½ pint. Add sugar, cinnamon and allspice. Boil to dissolve the sugar. Add just ripe, peeled mango halves, without the stone. Simmer 40 minutes. Leave for a couple of days before serving.

Spiced Brochettes of Ling

700 g / 1½ lb ling
1 tablespoon sunflower or
   groundnut oil
1 heaped teaspoon garam masala
3 teaspoons freshly ground
   coriander
1 teaspoon Mexican chilli powder
3 teaspoons freshly grated ginger
   root
1 clove garlic, crushed
sea salt
1 lemon
200 g / 7 oz goat's milk
   yoghourt
30 g / 1 oz flour
oil

Skin the ling and pull out any stray bones with tweezers. Cut the fish in 2.5 cm / 1 inch cubes. Heat the tablespoon of oil in a small pan, fry the garam masala, coriander and chilli powder. Mix the ginger, garlic, sea salt, lemon juice and yoghourt. Fold in the fried spice and beat in the flour. Put the fish in the yoghourt marinade and leave 1 hour.

Thread the fish on short wooden skewers. Barbecue or cook on a cast-iron grill pan. If you do the latter, put a sheet of oiled foil between the fish and the grill. Let the fish cool until tepid and serve with a green salad, tossed in a lemon juice and chive dressing.

Steamed Monkfish and Fettucine with Tarragon and Tomato Sauce

For the fettucine:
200 g / 7 oz bread flour
2 eggs (size 3)

For the sauce:
80 g / 3 oz diced onion
50 g / 2 oz butter
1 teaspoon dried oregano
2 heaped teaspoons chopped fresh
   tarragon
2 cloves garlic, finely diced
2 shallots, finely diced
700 g / 1½ lb tomatoes
700 g / 1½ lb monkfish
salt, pepper
chopped parsley

If you make pasta at home, either by hand or in a machine, prepare it with bread flour and two eggs. Roll the stiff dough as finely as you can and cut into narrow ribbons.

Sweat the onion in butter. Add oregano, 1 teaspoon tarragon, the garlic and shallots. Drop the tomatoes in boiling water for 12 seconds. Drain, skin, seed and chop the flesh. Add to the pan with herbs and onions. Cook to a pulp.

Cube the monkfish and steam 3 minutes over boiling water (slightly longer if necessary). Cook the pasta in boiling salted water 2 minutes and drain. Arrange on four dinner plates. Season the tomato sauce, mix in the monkfish and spoon on to the pasta. Sprinkle chopped parsley and remaining tarragon over the fish and serve.

Index